Judah Tyreman with Chris Tyreman

The Richest Kid in Babylon

AVARA BOOKS

Dedication

A big thank you to everyone who helped to put this book together. To all of my friends like Mrs. Haddock and Ms. Krimmel who proof read the invisible. A special thanks to Michelle Turgeon whose imagination came up with ways for a kid in ancient Babylon to make a buck, because if it was up to dad and me, we would still be trying to figure it out.

Introduction

This book came about after reading the old 1926 classic The Richest Man in Babylon. As a kid, even though the information was good, I found myself slugging along with the separate stories and old English, which was used to set the tone for the book.

It then hit me that a version for kids was the very thing that needed to extend the reach of this great information. So here appears the idea of that great book, mixed with a lot of my experience as a business owner, 1001 Arabian Nights, and Aesop's fables, which results in an easy read for kids 8-80 on accruing wealth.

Don't expect historically accurate material, as the value of silver and the like at that time is not correct.   Silver was so valuable in that day that you could buy 180 litres of barley for a single shekel which was only 11.33 grams. Rather than doing this, the amounts are imaginary and larger to give the story more flair.   After all, this is just another 1001 Arabian Nights, but for entrepreneurs and innovators.

Read on, have fun, and as my friend George Ure would say, "Write when you get rich."

Table of Contents

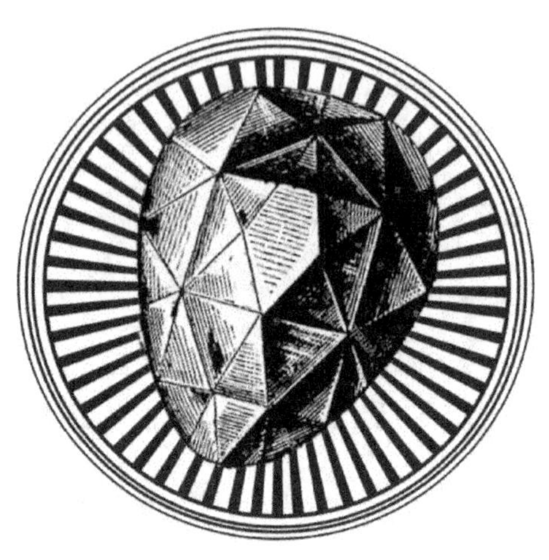

Chapter 1

A Gem of Great Price

In all of the great empire of Babylon, one man's name stood above all the rest when one spoke of the great merchants of the time. In his fifty some years, he had become one of the richest men of the era, acquiring fortunes in land, livestock and hard currency. It was said that his fortune was so great, that even the great scribes hired to establish the value of his holdings could never agree on its actual value.

Though his name was known, few men had actually ever met him, as his dealings carried him far and wide, and rarely to the city market. At least that is what they believed, but as truth and belief are not the same, he walked among their stalls and shops without their knowledge, always attentive to the business of the city and those who shopped for their needs there.

Today, it was not the merchants that caught his eye, but one who walked among the stalls. A young lad, perhaps twelve, or so, years of age, slipped almost unseen amid the overcrowded market.

He was ill dressed, but clean, and carried a small sack which he held by his side, and slowly, deftly filled with bits of food that he masterfully lifted from the tables as he slid between them.

Yet in all of this, he never touched any of the finery displayed among the stalls: no cloth or well woven items, no crafted pieces, or otherwise, that would have fetched a good coin, should he have desired to sell them.

It was this that caught the great man's attention.

The old man followed the lad, staying a distance away, so that he might not draw attention to himself and lose the boy.

Once the sack was half full, the lad exited the market and headed down one of the old backstreets, apparently unaware that he was being followed by the old man.

The young man entered an alcove through the street, where a small group of what appeared to be homeless children of various ages sat waiting. They jumped up at his appearance and began to circle him with excited voices and smiles beaming from their faces. Kneeling down he opened the sack, to divide out its contents fairly to each hungry child.

The old man watched from around the corner and listened.

The boy finished handing out the food, before assigning each of the children their tasks for the day. Some were to look after the younger, some to bring water, others, the older ones, were to try to find any work that might bring a copper coin or other wage, that they might buy other needs. None were instructed to steal.

The old man slipped into the shadows so the lad might not see him as he left the alcove. Then he followed the boy back to the market where he watched the young man approaching merchants, inquiring for work.

They brushed him away, returning to their trading as if he was invisible, an annoyance at best. Yet even though it would have been easy for the lad to pilfer from those tables, he touched nothing as he went.

The old man watched as the boy finally sat down in the shade under a tree by the market edge, that he might cool. Approaching, the old man sat next to him.

"It's a hard thing to find work in the market when one's back is not strong."

The lad looked over at him, "Why would someone such as yourself need work, sir?" Inquired the youth. "You wear garments of good value and your hands are not rough with the years of labor."

"That," replied the old man, "is not as curious as a young lad who seeks work when he could more easily steal what he needs while the merchants back is turned."

The boy frowned and picked up a handful of pebbles, to begin tossing them in front of him while he spoke. "It is wrong to steal for gain," he replied.

"Why?" replied the old man.

"Do you test me sir," he replied.

"In a way," he answered. "There are many reasons not to steal, I am curious what yours might be."

The boy finished tossing the last of the dirt and gravel from his hand, "because those who do, have no honor, and honor is the one thing that no man can take from me."

The old man raised his eyebrows. "But to steal to feed others is honorable?"

The young man looked at him, and then looked away, "You followed me out of the market and back. You are not a palace guard, nor one of the fat greedy merchants, so who are you?"

The old man leaned forward and rested his arms on his bent knees. "I am a man looking for a gem of great value that I might polish."

The boy frowned. "I do not understand your riddles."

The man faced the boy for the first time. "You feed children that are not yours and you only take enough, not more. You do not fill your own pockets, but by the work of your hand, if you can find it. You are an honorable thief, truly a very unusual gem, if I have ever seen one."

"What is it you want from me then? Do you want me to steal for you lest you tell the palace guards or the merchants?"

The old man shook his head and stood up, "The opposite my good lad. I offer you employment as an honest man should have, and as a bonus, food and clothing for those under your care."

The boy stood, "You jest with me sir?"

The old man turned to him. "Never. How long have you been on the street boy?"

"Two years sir."

"Then it has been two years longer than it should be. Tomorrow, at sunrise, be at the city gate, and I shall meet you where the elders gather." He reached into his purse and pulled three silver coins and handed them to the boy.

The lad's eyes widened even as a frown covered his forehead. "What are these for?"

"They are for items I need you to purchase if you wish employment with me." He motioned to the market, "Go and do your best to purchase a good set of clothes for yourself that you may be presented as a merchant's aide. I wish the best for the price. Do not dishonor me with poor quality upon your appearance.

The rest is to be spent supplying items for those who look to you. I expect all of it to be spent this day. There will be more tomorrow. Do you understand?"

The boy nodded, confusion still on his face.

"Until tomorrow then," finished the old man as he walked away.

"My Lord," yelled the young man, "who shall I say is my new master?"

The man shouted out his name without turning, "Ashar Ben Rakasha, the Judean."

The boy's eyes widened in shock as the aged figure was enveloped by the crowds of the market.

Chapter 2

The Beginning of Wisdom

It was one hour after the break of dawn, and the elders of the city began gathering at the gate while the youth who had preceded them looked on.

He watched as the crowds began to move in and out of the city gate, while the caravans that had arrived outside earlier, began unpacking their goods to sell to the merchants from the city.

While he was intent on the spectacle unfolding, Ben Rakasha approached him.

"Stand and present yourself young steward," he commanded quietly. The youth jumped to his feet and stood in front of his new master. Ben Rakasha looked over his outfit, tugged at several corners and nodded. "Well chosen. Now, tell me, are the children you oversee, well taken care of?"

The boy's eyes brightened. "They are good sir; they have eaten breads, fruit and even fish last night, and I had enough to replace some clothing that was needed."

"Very good." he replied. "Tonight you will do the same again, and it will continue, as you show yourself a good servant and steward of my coin. Now let us begin our work."

Ben Rakasha caught the attention of one of the elders and motioned him over. The elder frowned against the morning light as he approached, attempting to see who had bid him come.

His eyes widened as he recognized the young boy's master. "Ashar, is that you?" he asked, but once assured, he let out a shout of joy and they clasped their hands together. "It has been many months my friend. What brings you down to the market?"

Ben Rakash turned and motioned the elder to the boy, "This my good friend, is my new ward that I need to make contract with." The elder looked at the lad and bowed ever so slightly out of courtesy, "And what my young man have you done, that you might be extended the shelter of one so great as my friend here?"

The boy looked back, almost afraid, "I do not know good elder."

Ben Rakasha smiled, "I caught this young boy yesterday, feeding and caring for homeless children by the work of his own hand."

The elder raised his eyebrows, "How noble a gesture, your parents must be very proud to have a son such as yourself."

The boy opened his mouth not knowing what to say.

"His parents have recently passed away," interceded Ashar, "and as they had no other kin, I took it upon myself not to waste such a fine gem, but to bring the lad into training.

The streets are filled with those greedy who think they might fill their pockets with what I know, but without the heart this lad bears, it would be worthless to them."

The elder nodded, "So true; they can never understand that you can only keep what you give away. So my friend, how may I be of service in this matter?"

Ashar looked at the lad. "As I wish all of my dealings to be with honor, I am here to vow in your presence that I take this lad under my training, that my intent toward him to be known publicly by the elders."

The elder nodded and motioned the lad to follow. Taking him aside where the noise was less, he knelt down and spoke to the boy.

"What is your name young man?"

The lad looked up past the elder's beard and into his eyes, " It is Kasaf, lord."

"Do you understand who this man is, and his intent?"

Kasaf nodded quickly even though he did not.

The elder returned with the boy and wrote a contract of intent between the two. Then Ashar vowed seven times to keep the contract before the elders to make it legally binding.

When it was done, the elders bowed to Ben Rakasha as he bowed to them, and both he and Kasaf returned into the city.

Once again, they returned to the market and Ben Rakasha motioned for the boy to sit under the same tree as the day before.

He stared out at the bustle of commerce for a while, before speaking. "When I was your age, my family and I had just been brought to this place by an old king of Babylon named Nebuchadnezzar. At that time, he had conquered the land of Israel that I came from. I and all of the people of the land were brought here. That is why I am called a Judean. As you, I had nothing, and had to learn everything from the beginning. Today, I am honored and my wealth is beyond count, but even still, I lack many things.

Kasaf looked perplexed, "What could you lack my lord?"

"I lack a family, Kasaf. I lack friends who knew me when I had no money, and most of all, I lack a place to make sure that all I know will not be forgotten or misused."

"But you have some of the greatest wealth in the land, everyone knows of you, even the elders, you have many friends."

Ashar looked at Kasaf, "How many of them would die for me Kasaf and how many are friends only because of my wealth?"

Kasaf frowned again, "I had never thought of that my Lord."

"So, what do you now know that you did not?"

The boy thought for a moment, "Wealth cannot buy everything sir."

"Exactly," smiled the old man. "Once you have it, there are a great many things that you can no longer have. Your only friends are those you knew before. The only woman you can trust to love you, is the one who loved you poor. The more you have, the more time it takes to keep it. The richer you are, the poorer you can become."

The lad thought about what the old man said. "Then if it comes with such burden, why do men seek it with such heart?"

Ashar smiled sadly, "It is because one always wants a field ready for harvest over their own unturned plot of land, but they never consider the work that went into getting it there."

"Are you saying it is better to be poor?"

"No, I am saying that one must count the cost before beginning the journey. You must know why you wish this path and you must know the burden and responsibility of it, lest you harm both you and the world in your quest."

"Then what is the purpose of wealth sir, for I thought I knew, but realize I am but a fool?"

Ben Rakasha looked at him, "In this moment, Kasaf, knowing that, you may begin to become wise. For it is written, wisdom only begins, the day one knows they are a fool."

Kasaf looked confused, "I do not understand this, sir."

The old man smiled. "Many are those who believe they are wise, and because of this, they refuse council that goes against theirs. This makes them fools.

But if a man knows he has little wisdom, no matter how much he has, his is open to good council, and shall only increase in wisdom. Do you understand that?"

Kasaf nodded. "People who think they are wise pretend to know everything and therefore shall stumble in their foolishness. If one knows there is more to learn, then one will always seek council, and in the voice of many council, there is good advice."

"So, my young fool, are you ready to learn all of the ways of this old fool?"

Kasaf stood and turned to face Ben Rakasha, "This humble servant still does not understand why someone so great as you would do these things with me, but as the elders are witness, I shall strive to be honorable in everything that you teach."

Ben Rakasha smiled, "Then young Kasaf, let us begin with a story."

Chapter 3

The Four Silvers

"To answer your previous question," Ashar began, "what be the purpose of wealth? If we speak specifically of silver, it is a tool.

With that tool, one can lavish wealth upon themselves in waste, or use it to build. Those who seek to lavish it on themselves, rarely will ever be truly rich, or if so for a time, and they will end with little.

Those who use it to build, if done wisely, will not only change many things around them for the better, but shall still have more than enough for themselves."

"Is that what the elder meant when he said you can only keep what you give away?"

"I see you were listening," replied Ashar, "In a way yes, but I will explain all of this later. Today we start with a story, that you might learn about the different kinds of silver."

"There are different kinds lord?"

"Yes Kasaf, and most men can only see one. I will teach you about the four kinds that are invisible to most."

Ashar adjusted his position and leaned toward Kasaf, moving his hand across before them as if he drew back an invisible veil.

"In the days of old, there was a poor man named Zara, who desired to be rich. Yet no matter how he tried, he could not seem to accrue shekels in any great amount through his endeavors.

Life became so hard for him, that one day he went down to the ocean, ready to drown himself in despair.

As he sat on the sand, thinking about his dire action, an old blind beggar man came to him seeking a coin that he might purchase food.

Upon seeing him, Zara realized that he had no reason to be pitying his life, as the blind beggar's life was so much worse.

He was so thankful to the old man, that he untied his coin purse and handed it to him without counting it.

The blind beggar shook the purse and nodded. "Truly this is the most anyone has ever given me, for most give out of their surplus, but you have given me everything you had."

Zara was quite taken aback, for the beggar was right, "How can you know this old man?" he asked.

The beggar looked at him, smiled and pulled a glass lens from his robe. He handed it to Zara and bade him lift it to his eye.

Zara took the lens and looked through it at the old man. To his shock, he saw not the beggar, but a younger man, a prince dressed in the finest robes and jewels before him.

He jumped to his feet with a start, but as soon as he withdrew the lens, only the beggar was there.

"Look again," the beggar bade him, "but do not draw it away this time."

Zara once again lifted the lens to his eye, to see the other man.

"Who are you?" he asked trembling, "What kind of magic is this?"

The rich ruler before him spoke firmly, "The glass is not magic, Zara, this world is. For its ruler has many men under a spell of blindness. The lens you look through shows you what is real.

"Why do you show me this?" questioned Zara

"I show you this, because you freed yourself from the blindness when you gave me your purse," replied the rich stranger.

"How did my gift to you accomplish this?"

The rich man reached out and retrieved the glass from Zara's eye, and to Zara's astonishment, the visage of the blind beggar was gone, and only the rich ruler remained.

The ruler pocketed the lens and spoke. "The moment you ceased to think of only your needs and began to see the needs of those around you, in that moment you stopped looking inward and began to look outward.

You only needed the glass for a short time so that you would know what truth looked like. Now you have no more need of it. Now, look upon those who walk the sand."

Zara looked around him and noticed that people were walking along the beach, readying themselves for the day's fishing and trade.

Suddenly silver coins began appearing above their heads, only to fall to the sand, where they would sit for a moment, and then sink never to be retrieved.

The rich ruler waived his hand across the view in front of them.

"Now that you can see, I shall show you what most are blind to. Those coins which appear over their heads and disappear in the sand, are the ideas of these men. Things that they might create that would bring them hard silver.

But they are so busy running the path for themselves, that they take no notice of the coins, and they are lost forever, never to return. If they would stop and take them into their hand, they could better the world with what they could create.

This is the first kind of silver that is lost to those who seek only for themselves."

Zara stepped forward and picked up a coin, and an idea for repairing nets sprang to his mind. Another, and he saw a sail that would make a ship go faster. Each time he picked up a coin, an idea he had never had before popped into his head.

The rich ruler touched his shoulder and bade him follow. Zara walked with him off the beach and toward the city.

As they approached a field, the rich ruler motioned him to walk in it, and as Zara stepped, a silver coin appeared in his footprint.

'This," began the ruler, "is the second type of silver, for if you own land, it never goes away, never ages if it is cared for, and only increases in value.

One can build upon it or grow crops. One can even do nothing with the land and another will come and offer more then you paid for it. The man who owns land owns security."

They continued on their walk until they approached the market, and as they passed the stalls, Zara saw coins among the food on display, but not among the goods.

"Why?" he asked, "are there coins only among the food?"

The ruler picked up a cup, and it turned to sand and fell between his fingers. "That which is not food, has only the value that you wish to pay for it.

In hard times, its value is nothing. That which you can eat, the harder the times, the more value it has. Food is the third kind of silver."

When they had passed the market, they came to the junk dealer's booth, and Zara was amazed that silver coins lay all around on the floor of this shop even though it was not food.

"Why my lord," he asked, "are there silver coins among that which is thrown away, but not the new?"

The rich man picked up a piece and placed it in Zara's hand.

"To a blind man, these items are valueless. To one who sees, it is treasure. People surround themselves with that which is unnecessary, to impress those who do not care, rather than using that silver to create wealth.

They consume their future wealth with their present foolish wants and when these things no longer satisfy their wants, they grow bored and throw them away even though they still have good value. One may pick up another mans discard and sell it. This is the fourth kind of silver."

The rich ruler turned to Zara, "Do you understand now why you were poor?"

Zara nodded, "I believe so my lord. My focus was on making silver for myself, and just like seed, I ate everything I had so it always became smaller.

But if I look outward, and see not problems but look for answers, my silver will grow.

If I see treasure where others see garbage, I may pick up the silver they throw away, and if I stop feeding my empty desires, silver will only collect in my purse."

The rich man nodded and clasped his hands to Zara's. "What shall you now do with your new-found sight?"

Zara smiled, "I wish to go see the fisherman about repairing their nets."

The rich ruler bowed and walked away into the crowd, once again seeking alms from those around him, while Zara walked toward the beach a wealthy man.

Ashar finished and looked over at Kasaf. "What do you think of the story?"

Kasaf smiled, "I think it is a much better way of teaching than what the scribes do.

I remember everything, and because of that, every time I go to the market, or step on land, or see that which others throw away, I will see silver that I can collect. But more than that, I can with your leave, teach these things to the children you now feed, so that they too may see."

"Good." Ben Rakasha responded, "So now let us see if we can change the story into real silver.

Here is your task for the day. I want you to wander the market and see if you can find ways to use the four silvers to make the fifth one most can see. The one with the king's face on it.

Meet me here at the end of the day with your ideas and plans."

Ashar handed him several copper coins and a ring. "This is if you need food or otherwise when I am gone, I shall see you here at the end of day.

If anyone desires to cause you harm, you are to show them this ring and tell them you are my servant, and they shall leave you be. Do you understand?"

Kasaf nodded.

"Then be off with you and good hunting,"finished Rakasha, and with that he headed out of the market.

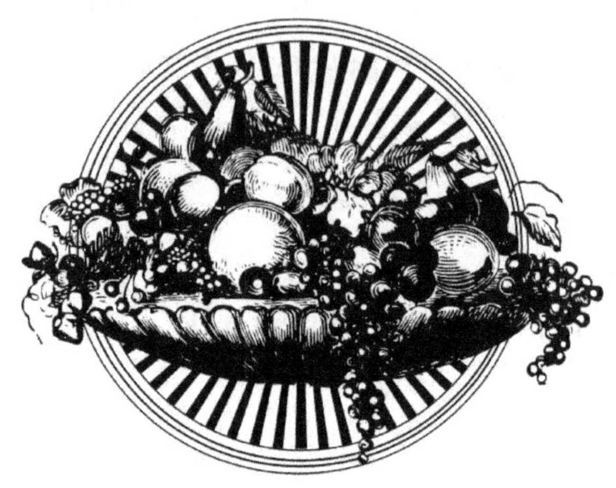

Chapter 4

The Fifth Silver

The sun was moving behind the taller buildings, stretching shadows into the market, when Ben Rakasha returned to find Kasaf awaiting him. He sat down next to him in his usual spot.

"So, my young ward, tell me of your silver."

Kasaf motioned out to the market. "I wandered the stalls, thinking at first that I might buy from one of the merchants, as I barter well, but I knew I had no place to sell.

I then considered looking for items that were of lesser value, that I might buy pieces from several merchants and maybe use them to build something different to sell, but again I was back at the first problem.

I thought that I might find what the merchants throw away, that I might turn it to profit, but others already do these things.

My final idea came from what you said in the story, that food was silver, and the scarcer it was, the more people would pay for it. This was the one that I could use."

"Hmm," said Ashar, "Tell me how."

"Here in the market," began Kasaf, "there is food a plenty, so one may haggle the price of bread and fruit down, as others are willing to deal. But outside of the city, the vendors don't go, as there is little profit away from the market."

"So how can you profit in this?"

"Here in the market, traders come from the four corners of the earth. Those from the north, trade with those from the south and so on. What if I bought fresh fruits from the south and then went out several miles to meet those caravans from the north.

They have been on a long journey and have not seen fresh food for many days. I believe I could sell to them at a higher price than I paid."

Ben Rakasha was impressed and showed it on his face, "How very shrewd for one so young. I am impressed. So how will you finance this venture?"

Kasaf drew himself up to begin. "Tonight, you shall give me silver to feed those in my care. They have enough from what you gave yesterday to eat in the morning.

I shall, with your leave, use that money to buy, tonight, what I need to take out to the caravans. The merchants give the best deals at the end of the day as they wish to rid themselves of old stock. Then in the morning I shall go out of the city to sell.

When I return, I will purchase what I need at the end of the day and have silver to spare if all goes well."

Ben Rakasha stroked his beard, "I cannot fault your idea young man. Proceed with your venture and let us see how it goes."

With that, he reached into his purse and withdrew two silver coins. "As you have no need of a new suit, it is only two coins tonight, but I am sure this will be more than enough for your venture."

Kasaf accepted the coins and quickly retreated backward into the market bowing toward Ashar as he went.

The morning found Kasaf carrying a sack full of fruits, walking the road from the city as the sun rose. The weight was more than he had bargained for, so it took longer than he had calculated to make the journey, but he was still early enough to precede the caravans.

Having achieved the correct distance, he sat down in time to see the first of the camels in the distance approaching on the road. He spread out a small sheet and set out some of the fruit in a pile that it might attract more attention.

As the first camel of the caravan was close enough, he ran twenty yards to meet it yelling greetings to the driver.

"Good morning kind sir." he called, "You look tired from your trip. May I suggest the purchase of one of my fine pomegranates to quench your thirst?"

The driver shook his head, "I shall soon be at the city boy, and I can bargain for all of the fruit I want."

"It is true sir," replied Kasaf, "but the city is still an hour away, and the sun soon shall be hot and for a small price, that hour may be spent in luxury instead of want, and the city prices are no better than mine."

A small smile came to the driver and he lifted his hand to motion the caravan to stop.

"What is your name boy?"

"Kasaf, sir."

"And who do you work for?"

"For myself sir."

"Indeed. Well Kasaf, I would be interested in one of your fine fruits and maybe my men also as they pass."

The driver turned and shouted some instructions down the line to which the others called back.

"Well my little man, it looks like we have some interest in your wares. Let me see one of your fruits."

Kasaf pulled the best from his bag and handed it to the driver. They bargained for a moment and agreed on a price. The driver reached for his coins, but Kasaf declined.

"No good sir, today for you this fruit is my gift to one who holds position such as yourself. Take it with my blessing."

The driver shook his head side to side. "Your name means silver in the Hebrew tongue boy and now I see why. With a head like yours, you shall have much of your namesake before long."

Again, the driver yelled to his men and then turned to Kasaf and winked. "It looks like many of us would like to travel in luxury for the next hour."

For the next several hours, as the travelers went, some purchased, some did not, but by the early morning, most of his goods had been sold. As the heat of the day had begun to climb, and the number of travelers declined, he decided to head back to the city.

As he passed through the market, he noticed his master already sitting by the tree. Kasaf ran to meet him and bowed.

"How have you fared?" asked Ben Rakasha.

Kasaf emptied his purse upon the ground and counted out the coins.
"I have three silver and five copper a profit for you on your two silver"

"No Kasaf," replied Ben Rakasha, "The profit is not mine, but yours to keep and use over and over each day. I wish you, with this work, to learn all involved in the creation of wealth. Continue as you have until your purse is full. When it is, we shall move to the next step."

Kasaf looked at him confused, "I do not understand. I am your servant and this is your silver and copper."

"And I sow it as good seed into your hands. Show yourself worthy of my choice."

Kasaf bowed again. "Good master, I shall do as you ask, but at least let me return five coppers each day, for the money lenders would charge this to me."

Ben Rakasha thought for a moment and then nodded in agreement. "I see your wisdom, as this is how business would be, so let it be."

Kasaf handed him the coins and put the rest in his purse. "What do you wish me to do with the rest of the day my lord?"

"I wish you to wander the markets and watch all of the transactions. Learn what makes a good merchant and a bad one. Store all of this in your mind day after day, so that when your time comes, you will not waste your wealth learning through mistakes. Learn rather through the mistakes of others and save the coins in your purse. We shall meet tomorrow at the same time as today."

Kasaf bowed again and ran off into the market.

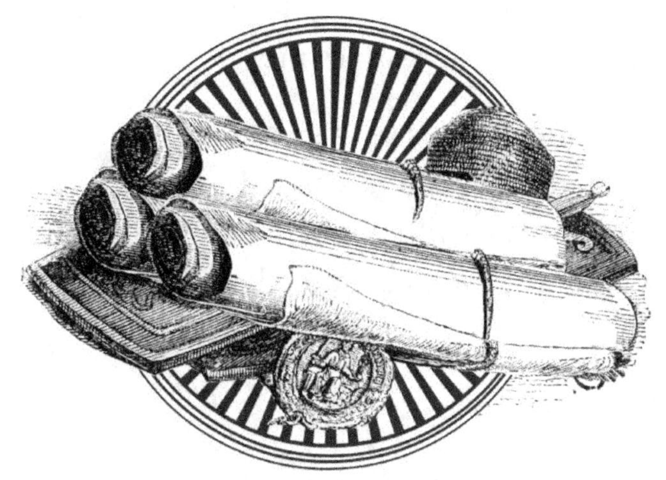

Chapter 5

Allahdan and the First Scroll

As mid-morning approached, Kasaf once again entered the city gates to find his master. As he expected, the old man sat under the tree waiting for him. Kasaf once again bowed and was bid to sit next to Ben Rakasha.

"How did you fare this second day Kasaf?"

Kasaf frowned, "Not as well as yesterday, there were less people on the road today and the clouds made men less heated, so my goods were not as appealing. Today I only have one extra silver and twenty-five coppers."

Ben Rakasha stroked his beard, "Still a fine return for a boy your age. There are men who work for hours in the hot sun for less."

"Do not think me unthankful my lord, I had merely wished to bring more honor to your faith in me."

Ashar put his hand on the boy's shoulder, "My young man, you were up before the dawn and carried a good weight along the road while most men still slumbered in their beds. Would that you had sold nothing, you had already brought me honor."

Kasaf forced a smile and pulled five copper coins from his purse to hand to his master.

Ashar looked at him, "Our deal was as the money lenders, how many of my shekels did you use for today?"

"One, my lord."

"Then the money lender only receives two coppers and a brass, not five."

Kasaf began to protest, but a look from Rakasha stopped him and as his master commanded, he gave him two coppers and a brass.

"Tomorrow," began the old man, "you shall no longer need to borrow from me. All the money you earned is yours to work as you see fit. Now, tell me what you learned of the merchants yesterday."

Kasaf set the coins back in his purse and tied it back to his belt. "I walked among the merchants yesterday to learn why some are more prosperous than others. I found it was a mix of things that made one more or less, the quality of the goods not-withstanding.

Those who did not smile or greet their customers did not do as well as those that did.

Those which were not confident of their product sold less than those who seemed to be.

Those who appeared afraid to approach possible customers did less in selling, and also in bartering, than those who were more confident."

"Good," replied Ben Rakasha. "Do you think that everyone who appeared confident really was?"

"I could not tell; they appeared to be."

"And those fearful, were they?"

"Yes, my lord."

"How do you know this?"

"For no one wishes to look afraid or without confidence, so they would not be pretending this, for it loses them silver."

Ben Rakasha nodded, "Now think about that, those who fear, are obvious, but one cannot tell if the confident are true, or hiding their fear. What do you learn from that?"

Kasaf thought for a moment, "If I appear confident, whether I am or not, others will not know. So, if I pretend to be confident, my sales will go up, my bartering will become stronger, and with that, my confidence will become real."

Ben Rakasha smiled. "This, my young ward, is a secret that most men do not know. They do not take stock of their appearance and manners before others. This by itself, will increase your silver if done properly."

"How do they learn such things my lord? Is there one who teaches?"

"Yes," replied Ben Rakasha, "Observation. You showed this by what you yourself noticed in one day. So, by sitting in the market, one can learn that which took others years to learn, in days."

"Then why do those poor in practice not learn these things?"

"Because they feel they are already fine merchants and they can learn no more from their competition. So, because of their false pride, they will stay poor. They instead blame other conditions on their lack. This goes back again to what you learned about wisdom. It only comes to fools.

So," he continued, "each time you learn a thing such as this, you must fix it hard in your mind. Each truth, such as this, is as if you had found a silver coin today, for if you take it to heart, it will place many coins in your purse that will never come to those who already think themselves wise."

Kasaf had realization, "So a man, or boy like myself, can learn all of the secrets to fatten a purse without cost, just by watching how others do, or do not do it."

"Yes. Those secrets are the difference between little or much."

"So true wealth is stored in your head and heart and if a man only acts on these secrets of silver, then it will supply all one needs."

Ben Rakasha frowned and stared at the young man.

"What is it master?"

"You are sure you are a boy, and not just a very small man in disguise? That truth Kasaf eludes men their whole lives and you learned it in an afternoon." Rakasha laughed, "Imagine what shall happen in a month."

"That was good then?"

"Not just good lad, as you said, it was silver. That, by the way, brings a story to mind, about treasure and riches beyond compare. Have you heard the story of Allahdan and the lamp?"

"Yes sir. Where one rubs the lamp and the jinn appears to grant wishes."

"That very one," replied Ben Rakasha. "I shall let you in on a secret, it was not a lamp that was sought. That is a change that came about through years of retelling. What was sought, was the vessel which contained the three scrolls of illumination.

With them it was said that every wish could be fulfilled, and that if desired, a man could rule the world should he read their secrets and understand what was written.

Now there was a mage at that time, who craved the secrets for himself. He was warned, on the map he had acquired showing where the scrolls were, not to touch the treasures of the cave, for one who did would never understand the scrolls. But, when the mage walked that very cave, he ignored the warning and took from the treasures in the room.

When he opened the scrolls and read them, they held only simple confusing texts, and realizing his failing, he replaced the scrolls and sought out one who could pass the test to seek only the scrolls.

By divination, he came across a young man whose name was Allahdan, who lived with his mother in near poverty as his father had died years before.

Taking the lad to the cave, the mage explained to him the task, and let him down into the cavern.

Even though he was surrounded by unimaginable wealth, Allahdan completed the task with honor and touched not of the treasure of the cave, but brought the scrolls to the mouth of the cave where he had been let down.

Before the mage would extend the rope, he asked Allahdan to read them up to him.   Allahdan opened the first and read to the mage the very words that the mage had seen with his own eyes.

The mage was enraged and accused Allahdan of having taken from the treasures along the path, and even though Allahdan denied such action, the mage rolled the stone back across the cave, to let Allahdan die while he found another to complete the task."

Ben Rakasha paused, "Now knowing there was not a lamp kasaf, is there anything you want to know?"

Kasaf looked at him and frowned slightly.

"I thought this was merely a tale, but you have asked me a question that reveals you know more.

If this then is more than merely a fable, I wish to know what was written upon the scrolls and not how Allahdan escaped his tomb.

I wish that I might understand the words written with the help of my master."

Ben Rakasha raised his eyebrows.

"May I test you then to see if you have taken from the treasure without knowing it?" he asked.

Kasaf looked confused, "I do not understand sir."

"When you take your fruit out in the morning to sell, do you eat of it at that time?"

"No," replied the boy.

"Why not, it is yours."

"Because I cannot sell what is in my stomach sir. After, when I feed the children what is left, then I partake."

"See how you only go for the goal, and not the treasure along the way. You might understand these scrolls after all."

And with that, Ben Rakasha reached into his robe and withdrew three scrolls of vellum and handed the first to Kasaf.

The young man took it and looked back at the old man.

"Are you saying these are the scrolls sir? Surely you jest with me."

"Do I?" replied Ben Rakasha, "Then open the first and see if one who does not touch the treasure along the way can decipher what it says."

Kasaf unrolled the old scroll to reveal the words on the skin.

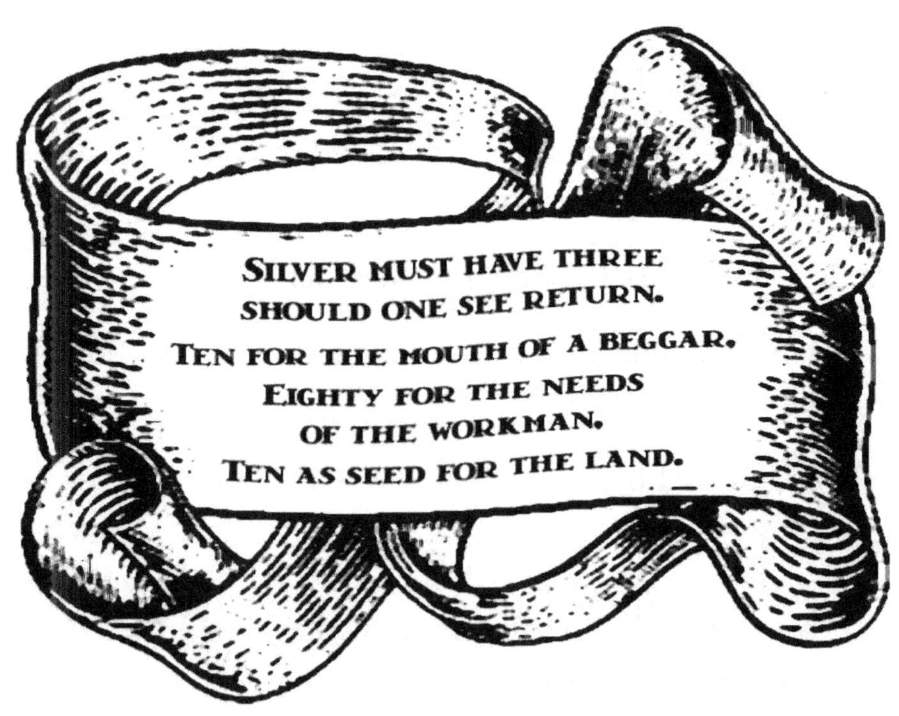

Ben Rakasha leaned toward him, "Can you read of this?"

Kasaf nodded, "My father taught me before he died."

"Do you have any idea what it means?"

Kasaf studied the words. "It says silver must have three, and there are three things listed below. That would mean that either each of these things must be done to have silver, or be done with silver, or both."

"Very good," responded Ashar, "Now can you tell me what the three mean?"

Again, Kasaf waited as his eyes scanned the words, letting them slowly sink into him.

"The mouth of a beggar seems easy, as one should always give to those who cannot work. The scroll speaks of a hundred silver. So, if you have one hundred coins, ten should go to those in need.

Eighty for the workman, would be those who worked for the silver, so eighty out of every one hundred the worker should keep for himself."

"And ten as seed for the land?"

"That one looks harder, but not if you read the words. It doesn't say seed for the land, but *as* seed for the land.

This means you should treat ten silvers out of every one-hundred as you would seed that would be sowed.

It means that you should set aside that ten to create more. If you use it to buy things right away for your wants, it would be like eating your seed, but if you sow it properly, like a crop, more silver will grow."

Ben Rakasha leaned back against the wall behind him and waited, not saying anything.

Kasaf waited and then began, "Was I right my master, or have I misunderstood?"

Ashar turned and looked at him, "I feel sometimes that I wasted so much of my life looking for someone who could understand those words. I have shown them to elders, many wise, and unwise, to scribes and religious men. Even to merchants and rich men, and none could fathom them.

Now I sit with a youth, a boy from the street who understands better than all of those learned men.

It is so sad that most confuse schooling with education. How many lives are wasted while they learn to walk the path of those whose feet have never trodden the road themselves."

Kasaf looked worried at his lord.

"You have done more than well young man; you understand the first scroll. This is the first set of truths that must be followed if a man wishes fortune beyond compare. How he applies this at the start of his journey, determines how his journey shall end.

Tell me then in simple terms how your money is to be divided?"

Kasaf sat up straight, "Ten percent for the beggar, eighty for the earner, ten to invest."

"Precisely," affirmed Ben Rakasha, "would that I could admonish you to begin this journey, but I have no need, as these things you already do.

Therefore, return to the marketplace and watch again, for tomorrow you shall open the second scroll."

Kasaf stood quickly and bowed to Ben Rakasha and began to run off.

The old man bid him to stop. "You forgot your silver for the children today."

Kasaf returned and took the two coins respectfully, "Thank you my Lord." He bowed again quickly and disappeared into the crowd.

Chapter 6

The Second Scroll

It was the finish of a particularly good morning for Kasaf as he entered the city.

On the third day, his profit for the day exceeded three silver coins and more. He set down next to Ashar and proudly displayed them, his face beaming with a grin.

Ben Rakasha nodded, "It is a wonderful feeling to watch one's purse fatten with the jingle of silver. You do well with your idea. Have you thought of ways to grow your profits?"

Kasaf brightened even more. "It is as if you read my mind my lord. Just this morning as I walked out, I considered that I was limited in how much I could carry each day.

I wondered if adding bread and other items could increase what I sell for the day, but the weight is too much.

I therefore have considered renting one of the market donkeys for the morning. After they are unloaded, they stand all day at some stalls.

I believe I might find that Akim, the merchant who sells me much fruit, might be very open to lending his donkey to me in the morning. The more I can carry, the more I would buy. It would be to his advantage to create such a deal and at no extra cost to me.

To add to this, I could bring one of the older children in my care with me. I can train him as I do, and he can speed up the service along the caravans. Then when he is older, I can send him and another to the other side of the city to do the same thing.

Soon my lord, we could feed ourselves without the need of your coins.

Ben Rakasha nodded approvingly, "Well thought out. I cannot find fault in your idea. Let me know tomorrow how it goes and we can discuss ways to increase even those ideas. Now", continued Ben Rakasha, "Do you remember yesterday's scroll?"

"Yes," answered Kasaf. "Ten percent for the beggar, eighty for the earner, ten to invest, and today I even had enough to give to those at the gate who needed coin"

"And what did you learn from this action my young man?"

Kasaf smiled, "That I am no longer poor my lord. Three days ago, I felt as if my struggle had no hope, yet within three days I now have silver, my children are fed, and I give at the gate as only a rich man can."

"And how does it feel to give?"

"All the emptiness that was my heart and all of the anger of my lot is gone, and my heart is full, for I have changed the world today of those in need."

"Excellent Kasaf, the first scroll now lives within your heart. Use them and teach others. Now, the second scroll."

Ben Rakasha drew back the edge of his robe and slowly pulled out the second parchment. He handed it to Kasaf and bade him unroll it. It was drier than the last one, and he moved slower for fear that he might damage the vellum as it came apart.

He laid it out upon his legs and let his eyes slowly wander over the script, allowing each word to sink into his thoughts, hoping that this one would be as easy as the first, so that he might please Ben Rakasha.

Ashar waited until the boy had time to finish the piece, not wanting to make him feel pushed to answer quickly.
"What do you think?" he asked.

Kasaf began to read the first line.

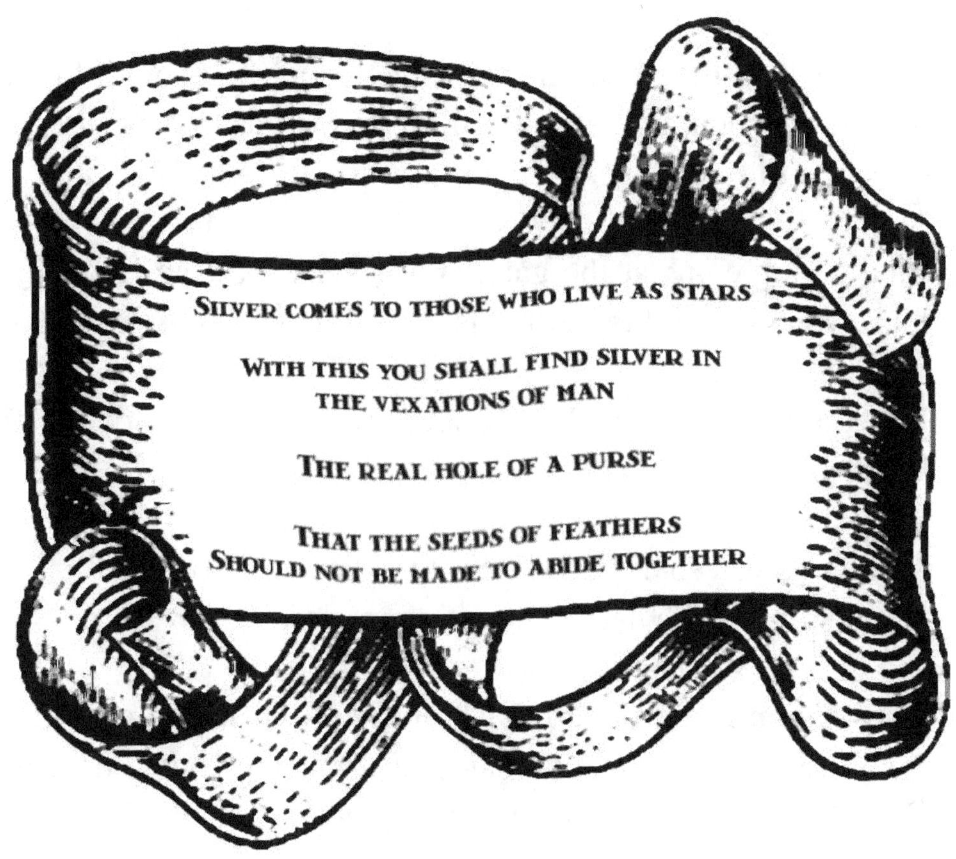

"Silver comes to those who live as stars."

Ashar waited, "Your thoughts?"

Kasaf talked it out slowly, "A star is a light in an ocean of darkness. No matter how dark the night, you can always see it in a clear sky.

It gives direction to those on the sea, lets those who watch seasons know the coming of the floods such as the Nile. It always pours out, and never takes anything in return.

If I look at it like that, one who lives as a star, should do those things. We should pour out to those around us in darkness, give direction to those lost.

Like giving coins at the gate, and never expecting return from those you give to. I think that is how you become a star."

Ben Rakasha nodded. Very good, that is the truth of the first line. Now try the next one."

"With this you shall find silver in the vexations of man."
Kasaf stopped. "What is a vexation my lord?"

"A vexation is a problem that follows you that you never seem rid of. Like a lazy son, or a nagging woman, or a callous man. Or in your case, a hot sun at mid-day with no shelter."

"Then this would be what you taught me before. I take food out to the caravans, and make silver from what vexes them, the long journey and dried out meat full of worms.

So, if I am a star and always pouring out, it allows me to see what vexes others because I care to fix it.

When I see these problems, I can find an answer, and make silver at the same time, which I can use to help others and myself."

"Exactly!" yelled Ben Rakasha startling the boy. "I am sorry my lad, but I have never heard anyone put it quite so well as that. I wish I had a scribe so I could have written that down.

Well, no matter, I'm sure you know what you said and could say it again. Now I really don't want to push you, but the next one is my favorite and I am curious just how far that head of yours can go. What do you think the next line means?"

Kasaf read it out loud, "The real hole of a purse." He paused and looked back over the scroll and thought again of the line.

"If I live as a star, I can find the real hole of a purse. Does it mean the hole at the top, or what happens if your purse has a hole at the bottom?"

"Is the position of the hole what causes money to come out?" asked Ashar.

"Coins can leave for many reasons my lord," answered Kasaf.

"They can be removed by the bearer of the purse, they can fall out from a hole, or be taken by a thief."

"Very good, but can a man be both the bearer of his coins, and a thief?"

"Lord?"

"Think about it for a moment and then answer the question."

Kasaf considered what was asked. "If one has a need, then one should remove from their purse. To buy something of little value out of want, rather than need, is foolish, as your need for tomorrow might not be met.

In that way, you might say that fools steal from themselves, when they buy what is not needed."

"So where is the real hole of a purse?"

"If one looks at it in that way, the real hole of a purse, is in one's heart. If we purchase to fill the emptiness there, then our purse shall always be empty.

Is this why the purse of a poor man and a well-to-do man are both empty at the end of each month?"

"Yes," replied Ben Rakasha, "The rich person's desires increase with their wealth, which is why many who become rich, become poor again.

A man is either lord of his desires and emotions, or they be lord of him. Emotion is a beautiful servant, but a hard task master."

"So again," added Kasaf, "if one lives as a star, then the hole shall disappear, but if one only tries to fill the hole with things they might purchase, they are like the night sky, which eats of the star's light and returns nothing."

"Yes, one who looks outward, lives a life desiring to create. This action of creation fills the hole, for the hole can only be filled with personal prestige that comes from creating.

If one purchases to pretend that they are something they are not, that cannot fill the hole, and in fact it makes it only bigger. Many borrow from the money lender to buy what they have not earned.

The money lender lets people pretend they are something they are not. Remember Kasaf, if possible, touch not the money lenders purse, for the man you owe money to, owns you"

"Is that why you do not wear the garb of your stature, but only one of good quality, and why no jewels adorn your hands?"

"Yes Kasaf, my treasure is piled high in my heart and resolve. I have no need to prove anything to anyone. Remember, it is better to walk in the clothes of a pauper and have coins in your purse, then be attired as the richest king with a grumbling belly.

One of the greatest secrets to gaining wealth, is to have coins leave your purse slower than they go in.

Take for example your idea of using a donkey each morning.

You have enough silver that you could own one, yet in wisdom, you thought to ride for free. To own it, people might speak better of you, seeing that you now ride your own instead of Akim's. So why not own?"

"What people think of me does not fill my purse. If I drove a chariot down the street and made people step aside, and it was covered in the finest jewels, none of that creates more silver.

To add to this, the horse must be stabled and fed and cared for, and soon my purse would be empty.

It is the same for the donkey. I have all of the luxury of the owner, without the cost. Until owning the donkey exceeds that value, I should never own"

"Exactly," responded Ben Rakasha, "and now you understand the full meaning of the second riddle. Now finish the third."

"If I am a star, then the seeds of feathers should not be made to abide together. That one is easy my lord. A week ago, at the market, one of the stalls was bumped during a scuffle between two men. They knocked over a basket of eggs and smashed them.

Answer…do not keep all of your shekels in a single investment."

Kasaf looked proud of himself.

Ben Rakasha shook his head and laughed.

"So then, as you most likely expect me to say, your job for today is as yesterday, take what you now know and return to the market to see how you can apply it. Tomorrow, we shall open the last scroll."

Ben Rakasha handed him two silver coins and bid him away.

Chapter 7

The Third Scroll

Kasaf was earlier than the day before, excited with new news for his master. He had expected to wait, but Ben Rakasha was already there awaiting him. Kasaf bowed and quickly sat beside him.

"I am so glad you came early my lord, for I have wonderful news of how I used the scroll to increase my silver."

"Do tell my young man," retorted Ashar.

"The scroll said that one who lives as a star shall find silver in the vexations of man. Well it was not a man, but a servant girl that I met in the market.

She was trying to purchase a ring for her mistress that had been lost earlier. She had been sent to the market and was trying to bargain with a seller but to no avail, as he knew that her mistress had much silver.

She walked away without buying it, trying to find another at a lower price, but again to no avail.

Then an idea came to me, a silver coin over my head, but I did not let it fall to the sand.

I approached her and offered to buy the ring for her and if I could purchase it lower than what she wished, then she would pay me half the difference.

She was not convinced, but had nothing to lose, so with her hidden from the merchant I haggled with him.

As he knew not of my wealth, the ring's price was much lower. I told him I would give him half what he asked. He told me to not waste his time and to come back when I had silver.

I told him it was a pity, that I had seen him lose his last sale for it and now he would lose mine and I opened my hand to show the shekels as I walked away.

I was not ten feet when he called me back and began haggling again.

When it was all said and done, I made twenty copper for just a minute's work, and the servant girl will have a mistress who is pleased with her.

From now on, when she needs of the market, she said she will have me do the purchases for her. So not only do I have my mornings coin, but coin from the market also.

From now on, as soon as you bid me to the market, I shall watch for others who need such service. I shall increase my silver much faster now just as the scroll said."

Ben Rakasha's smile grew as the boy spoke. "Ah Kasaf, if only I had been as wise as you when I was your age, I could have been king by now.

I thought I did well, but now I almost feel I wasted years of my life. With that, let us not waste anymore of yours then!"

The old man pulled the last scroll from his robe and set it in Kasaf's hands.

The boy slowly unrolled it and began to read.

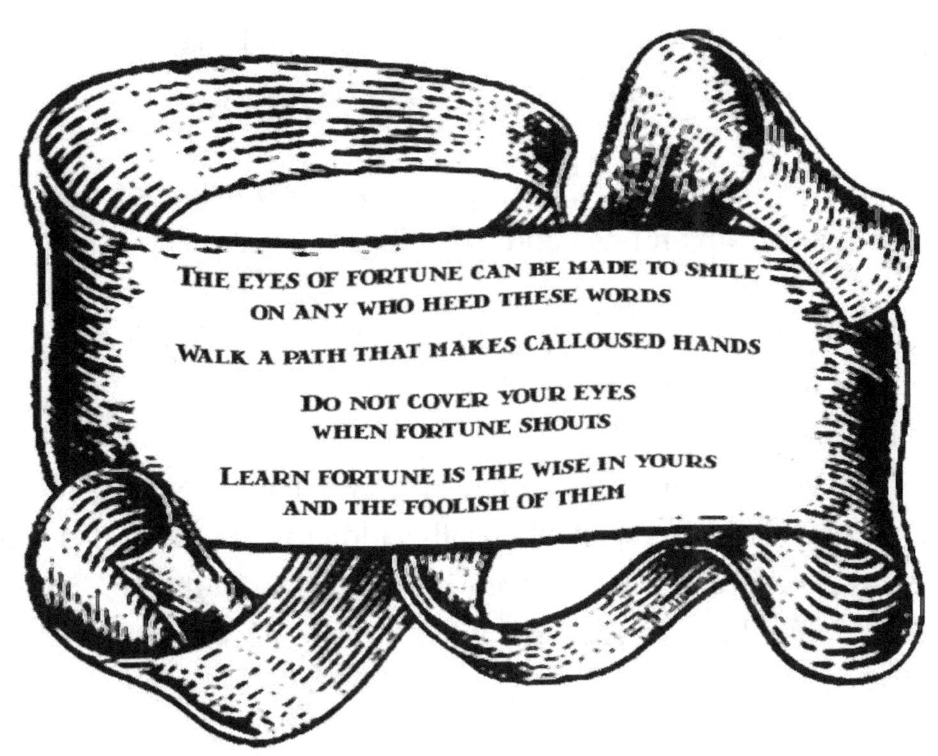

"The eyes of fortune, my lord?" Kasaf questioned, "Does it mean like a god who looks down on mankind?"

The old man smiled wryly. "Many are those who believe that the gods choose to benefit a chosen few and plague the rest.

This is how people account for good things or bad things that happen."

"Why would people wish to serve such gods then?"

"You do not feel the need to serve the gods of this land as many do?"

Kasaf shook his head, "I see only wood and metal, and those who make profit from these foolish ideas.

Fortune as you have shown me comes from knowledge and action, not from an false god."

"So why then do people pay heed to these deaf gods that they made with their own hands?"

"I believe, my lord, it is because they wish an excuse for not taking action. They can blame the idol for anything that goes wrong, and pretend it was their idol if it goes right, so they can tell people how much smarter they are for having a more powerful god.

If they do what is wrong, they go to the idol and offer a sacrifice to be forgiven rather than going to those they have wronged to make it right.

They never have to be accountable for their actions, and only pretend they believe what they did was wrong.

They use the false gods to let them sleep at night believing they are good men when their hands rush to do evil to the poor, the widows and the orphans."

"So, if you do not believe that this speaks of a god, what do you think it means?"

"I think it means that a wise man knows that fortune can be brought by action, for the three that are listed below tell us you can move the eyes to bring fortune to you."

"Continue then."

"Walk a path that makes calloused hands, obviously means to do something over and over until you have mastered it.

A person who is good at something will appear to an untrained person as having fortune smile more often upon them."

"Correct," affirmed Ben Rakasha, "As a man practices his art, it becomes easier, and the better he is at his craft, the more who will seek what he makes.

To the unpracticed he will appear to have an easier time of life, for they have not seen his endurance to his trade, only the outcome."

"So," replied Kasaf, "whoever wrote these lines, wrote it so that those who believe in their idols will never be able to understand what it says, as they will believe it speaks of a god that they need to serve."

"Yes. Only when a man frees himself of the belief that he does not have choice, can he begin to change his life.

While we blame the gods, or fortune, or those who raised us, or those who wronged us, we are shackled to a lie that we want to believe. Only when we cut free of this idea, can we begin to change.”

“And how might one free themselves my lord?”

“With the greatest gift that our maker has given mankind - with choice.

You simply say…No more! From this day forward, it does not matter who I am, or what I believe about myself, you simply choose.

Choose to let go of a past that no longer exists. Choose to live as a star and follow the rules of silver and when you are done, when your life has been spent to its full upon the earth, none of what shackled you before will matter.

You are who you are because of the path of your life. You can either use these events to fly, or to sink among the sand of despair.

Choose.”

Kasaf stared at Ashar for a moment. “So, one who believes in the fates can never succeed as one who believes that your fate is what you make it.

One who believes in fate, does not prepare, but the one who does prepare, is ready for what comes next. That is what the third line is speaking of then.

When fortune shows itself, it requires change in us, just like I had to walk far from the city to find those to buy from me.

Slaves do not like change, so they will close their eyes to fortune when a great opportunity presents itself because they are not ready for what it requires of them.

The King is ready because he has practiced readying himself for what might come. Like a star, he looks outward and forward and so he sees fortune approaching."

"Exactly Kasaf. Now let me tell a story.

There were two brothers who were twins, raised in the same house, in the same way all of their life. But the one brother had the soul of a ruler, and the other the soul of a slave.

The ruler believed that his hands dictated his fate, and though things might go wrong, planning could lower the chances of an evil wreaking havoc in his life.

The other brother who had a slave's soul chose to believe he had no say over his fate, and was resigned to accept whatever evils might befall him.

Each of them built a house, an exact copy of the other. The ruler, knowing that fires could destroy all of his hard work, placed barrels of water and pails around the rooms and outside of his house, while his brother the slave did not.

One night, an evil man who hated both of the brothers, set fire to each of their homes. The brother with the soul of a ruler quickly doused the fire with the waters, but the slave's house burned to the ground.

The ruler continued to enjoy his house, while the slave hated that the fates had smiled on his brother and not him. Thus the slave's belief embittered him and those around him for the rest of his life."

Ben Rakasha finished, "So tell me, young Kasaf, what do you think the teaching of the story is?"

"It is the fourth line in the scroll master; learn that fortune is the wise in yours and the foolish of them.

It speaks again of believing in choice. The slave chooses to believe in fate, and loses everything, while the ruler chooses choice. Then, rather than accepting that the fault was his, the slave hates his brother for being "chosen" by the fates to succeed."

Ben Rakasha leaned forward, "Why would a man be so foolish Kasaf?"

Kasaf shook his head for it made no sense to him.

Ben Rakasha explained. "The greatest gift man has is choice.

What most do not understand is there is a second great secret hidden in the first. Not choosing, is a choice. You can never escape being made to choose.

And in that, there lies a third hidden secret. The secret that can turn any man to wealth.

The secret is, no one ever fails. They only choose actions which gain silver, or lose it."

Kasaf frowned.

"I shall put it a different way so that your eyes might see. If a man wishes to pass a test, but does not study, or studies in such a way that he might not remember that which he needs to, he will not have the answers for his test. Correct?"

Kasaf nodded,

"So did he fail," continued Rakasha, "or, did he actually succeed in *not* passing his test?"

Kasaf's eyes lit up, "I understand. If a man is going on a journey and walks the path to his destination he goes forward.

If he turns around and walks back, he is further from his goal.

In both he successfully walks, but only one gets him closer to where he needs to be."

"Yes," affirmed Ashar. "So, what does that mean for any man?"

"It means if you do not like what happens to you, change what you do. You are where you are, but you can choose from this moment on to be elsewhere. If a man follows the rules of paupers, he shall become poor. If he follows the rules of silver, wealth shall chase him down."

Ben Rakasha smiled, "Once again, young man, you display wisdom beyond your years. These things of which you speak, you yourself have done, and silver flows into your purse. Now with that, I bid you leave, as I have other things which call me.

Today I give you a purse of silver for the needs of those beneath you as I must journey for some days. When the purse is empty, I shall be sitting here again to await you.

Continue in what you have learned, and when I see you again, we shall see how you and your purse fared."

With that, Ben Rakasha reached into his robe and drew out a leather purse which he gave to Kasaf. He stood, and this time he bowed lightly to Kasaf and walked off into the crowd.

Kasaf watched him leave and vowed in his resolve that he would do his master proud. He then worked his way into the crowd, to find more who needed his service, his eyes open to see any silver coins that might suddenly appear above his head.

Chapter 8

The Magic Carpet

A full moon passed, until the purse was empty, and as his master had bid him, Kasaf returned to the tree and waited.

Approaching, he bowed as Ben Rakasha bid him to sit.
"It is good to see you again young Kasaf. Tell me how the month has treated you."

Kasaf pulled back the edge of his robe to remove a much larger purse and placed it into the hands of Ben Rakasha. The old man felt the weight in his hands and smiled.
"What is its total young man?"

Kasaf smiled, "Sixty-two silver coins and twenty-five copper from the sales outside of the city, forty-two silver and fifteen copper from helping people purchase in the market.

This, after paying five silver and ten coppers out on expenses. One to the oldest of the children in my care for helping along the city roads with the traders, two as a gift to Akim for the use of the donkey, and the rest to rent a small area for the children to sleep at night. That does not include the tenth which went to those in need at the gate."

Ben Rakasha opened the purse and lifted the silver in his hand. "I am very impressed young Kasaf. This is an excellent profit for a man, never mind a boy of your age. So, tell me, you have had a month; have you learned anything that you wish to share with me?"

Kasaf nodded, "I have watched the merchants and people among the market as they buy and sell, and I have added to my knowledge of how best to increase my silver as I deal among them.

For as was written on the scroll, one must make themselves ready, so they do not close their eyes when fortune shouts, so I have spent my time learning of the qualities of the merchants' wares.

The food dealers I had already known, so I turned my attention upon the others such as the blade merchants and those who sell metal wares, that I might learn of their trade. This, my master, was the wisest of choices, for just as the scroll said, fortune shouted toward me, and I was ready."

Ben Rakasha saw the smile begin on Kasaf's face.
"This then," began the old man, "must be the *real* story of your month, for you have held it back until the last."

Kasaf nodded and retrieved another purse from his robe and handed it to Ashar, as if it had no weight. When he released it, it pulled the old man's arms to his lap.

An expression of shock appeared on Ben Rakasha's face and he turned to look inquisitively at the boy.

"What have you here lad?" he whispered.

Kasaf motioned for him to open it. Ashar drew open the pouch to reveal it full of many silver shekels. He looked up at the young man.

"How much?"

Kasaf's face broke into a full smile, "Two hundred and eleven shekels, after feeding many poor at the city gate"

"But this is not from your regular affairs?"

"No, this is the shout of fortune, and I stared her right in the face and I did not blink!"

"Then tell me lad of this great windfall!"

Kasaf drew in a deep breath. "As was usual, about three and a half weeks after I saw you last, I was out upon the road in the morning selling, when two men from the south road approached. The older of the two looked sad and worried.

He stopped and asked me who my master was, and if he was interested in picking up all of his wares at a very low price. I asked him why he must release them, and he told me that the other man with him was a messenger who had come from his city with the news that his father had fallen ill and that the gods might come for him.

The wares that he had weighed much, and he needed all speed to return home. I told him I could purchase for my master and asked to see his wares.

He looked unconvinced because of my age, but he opened one of his packs and withdrew a beautifully crafted long knife. Had I not followed your advice and prepared myself, I would not have known its value, but having studied those in the market, I was able to know of its worth.

I told him the quality was excellent and asked to see the rest. Again, for my age, I could see he felt it was a waste of time, so I withdrew a silver coin from my purse and gave it to him saying if I was lying as to my intent, he could keep it.

Now whether he thought me a fool, or believed me I do not know, but they unloaded his burden and opened the pieces. I looked them over and realized what good quality they were and asked his price. He asked for fifty shekels for the lot.

I was stunned that he asked so little and asked why he would let them go at that price. He told me that his love for his father exceeded anything that silver might buy, and it was still more than if he just threw them by the road. All he asked was enough so that he could buy enough metal to begin again.

I inquired if the others of the caravans might buy it, but he had asked and they all said their silver was contained in their goods and they would buy at the end of the day, but he could not risk the time.

He then asked a fifth of their value that he would have asked from the merchants in the city. I knew I could sell them myself in the market at eight times what he asked, keeping all of the profit for myself as I had the luxury of the time he did not.

I told him I would purchase all he had, but not at the price he asked. Should he wish me to take his goods, it must be for twice the amount.

The man looked confused and asked why I would offer one hundred silver. I explained to him two things; one, that his work was worth more than what he asked, and second, that I could not dishonor my master by acting as a thief.

For no man should ever take advantage of one who must sell when he is in need. With that I gave him almost all that I had, and after transferring his handiwork to my donkey, they hurried off.

Immediately I went to the market, and over the next three days, I quickly found homes for each of his fine pieces, for I could sell them at less than the other merchants and still take great profit.

So, because I was ready for the shout of fortune, I made two hundred silver, almost twice what my other labor of a whole month produced."

Ben Rakasha placed his hands together and bowed lightly to Kasaf. "My young man, you do me proud with all you have done. You have applied yourself diligently to your studies and have been rewarded in their craft. So, you are ready for more."

Kasaf smiled back. "I have waited all of this month, that I might learn more. For if I have increased my purse this much with just the beginning, I can only imagine what more shall come with the secrets you entrust to my hand today."

Ben Rakasha stood and bade the young man arise and follow. They walked quietly through the market until they came to a booth which sold imported carpets. The old man bent down to put his face closer to Kasaf's while he pointed to the well woven one at the edge.

"Do you see that one?" he whispered.

Kasaf nodded.

"Go touch it and feel the quality and compare it to the others around it. Check the tightness of the weave, the color of the dyes, and see if any of the color has faded from its time in the sun."

Kasaf went forward and spoke with the merchant who opened it for him to inspect. The merchant explained to him everything he knew about it and bid him feel it before rolling it up again. Kasaf returned to Ben Rakasha.

"It is one of the finest I have ever seen my lord. The shop master says it hails from the east where they produce these carpets in ways we do not here."

Ben Rakasha pointed back at the carpet. "There is a legend that it was a carpet exactly as that, that a prince named Hasan sat upon, and with it, he was able to fly to another land."

Kasaf smiled. "So now you shall teach me with this legend of the flying carpet my lord? Even before you tell it, I know the children will love this story tonight."

"Well then," smiled Ashar, "First I shall tell you that this was no story, but it actually happened. Let us go back to the tree and its shade where I might tell it to you"

Kasaf frowned as they walked, "You toy with me my lord. Am I to believe that flying carpets are real?"

"In a way." replied Ashar, "As in Allahdan, where there was no lamp, in this story, again slight adjustments are made, for people change stories as they are told over and over. In this same way, prince Hasan was real, as was the carpet, and he did 'fly off' to the land it was made from, but not the way it is told."

They approached the tree and sat down.

"As I said, a long time ago, there was a prince name Hasan from a kingdom much like this. Hasan cared for his people and wished to increase how well they lived, but there was a limit to how much silver one could make, as the people were poor, and the kingdom had not many resources to sell.

One day he walked through the market in disguise that he might observe his people. There, Hasan came across an old man who had come to beg for alms. The old man unrolled a carpet that was upon his shoulders and sat upon it to ease the pain of sitting on the rocky ground.

Immediately the carpet caught Hasan's attention, for it was well woven and without tatter and with pattern of great work. Hasan approached the old man and handed him some coins. He asked the old man where he had come upon the carpet, and the beggar explained that it was his father's, from many years ago, and a land far east.

Hasan asked if he might examine it for another coin. The beggar eagerly jumped up and allowed the disguised prince to sit and examine it. Hasan had never seen anything like it. The color was still very visible and the material more tightly woven and finer than he had ever seen, and as I said before, with many patterns mixed throughout.

He asked the old man if he would be interested in selling it. The old man was not sure, as it was one of the last things of his family.

Hasan said he understood and offered the beggar fifty silver shekels for it. The beggar thought the prince was trying to make a fool of him, but the prince pulled out his purse and counted out the silver.

The beggar took the coins and bowed down to the ground in front of the prince, thanking him with great joy, for now his needs were taken care of for the rest of his life.

The prince then took the carpet back to the palace and bid his servants to clean it. They carefully washed and dried it and brought it back to him.

The value that the prince thought it had before was nothing compared to now. The colors were dark and rich and gold and silver threads were woven though out the pattern. Even after years of use, the carpet looked as if it was almost new.

The prince had never seen anything like this and became very excited. He took it and showed it to the king and his advisers, all who were astonished at its quality and beauty.

The prince had a plan. He bid his father to let him take a group of men wise in their trades, who would leave at once to find where the carpet was made. Hasan believed that the many secrets of how such was made, brought back to his city, would kindle many types of work and trade that would bring prosperity to the land.

The king agreed, and that night the prince collected all the men and silver he might need, and the next morning, they flew off to the east to seek the carpets creators."

"Ah," said Kasaf, "Now I see, he flew off *after* he sat on the carpet, became he flew off *on* the carpet."

"It does make a better story does it not?"

"It does, but if you lose the point of the story, it steals many things from those who listen."

"And that young Kasaf is what happens when people become more interested in entertainment over attainment. The lazy wish their ears tickled, whereas the industrious wish that tickle to be silver upon their palms."

"So, what happened with prince Hasan, my lord?"

"To make a story short, the prince found where the carpet was created, and he and those with him purchased the secrets of its manufacture, studied many months with the men from the east, and brought all of this knowledge back to his city.

Once he arrived, Hasan brought together the best artisans and spinners and dyers of cloth and taught these secrets to them.

Soon there was need for silver and gold threads to be manufactured, and minerals to be mined for dyes, and the list went on and on. Different kinds of business sprang up to supply these needs all over the city.

It was not just rugs that were created, but beautiful cloths and tapestries, and many things of beauty. When word of these amazing things began to spread, merchants began coming to the city from all over the land to trade for these items, and in turn, the city was flooded in the years to follow with many goods they had never seen before.

Wages went up, many jobs were created, and the city began to flourish as people moved in from all over. Soon the city which had barely been getting by, became a center of trade and commerce. All this, because the prince had revived the art of innovation."

Ben Rakasha smiled as he finished, "That, my young man, is the real story of how a magic carpet brought wealth to prince Hasan and all of his people."

Kasaf clasped his hands around his knees. "How strange to think that one carpet could change the fortune of a whole land, and even more, that the beggar had been sitting on the greatest of treasures his whole life and was without coin."

Ben Rakasha nodded, "Such are the fortunes of the sighted and the blind. One man sees a dirty carpet, one man sees unlimited wealth."

"So, then I am to assume that I am now to find my own magic carpet and using the secrets you have taught me, and my silver, I shall create wealth not just for me, but those around me."

"It is a great task that I put toward you this time. What do you think of its scope?"

"I think that it both excites and terrifies me my lord. For to turn the carpet into treasure gives not a quick return as the selling of my fruit, but requires investment, wisdom, and time before I see a return."

"So, what law of fortune might you call that?"

Kasaf thought. "I would say that great return requires great investment and risk."

Ben Rakasha nodded again. "Well spoken. You will now have to wager your hard-earned silver toward potential gain. It does not have to be all of it, but it might."

Ashar stood. "Now once again my young man, I must leave you, for I only had a short time to be here today, and my affairs call me away for a long time. It shall be twelve moons before I see you again".

A look of sadness came over Kasaf's face.

"Do not look sad my young Kasaf, you are now at the age, and knowledge, where people will see you as a young man. Care well for those beneath you and continue to train them well."

Ben Rakasha reached for his purse, but Kasaf stopped him.

"Not this time my lord, I now have enough silver, even with what comes, to feed and care for all of us. If I am as you say, then today I stand on my own to care for my family. I shall look forward to seeing your face soon."

Ben Rakasha clasped his hands to Kasaf and bowed lightly toward him and Kasaf responded the same.

"May he who gives us life," began Ashar, "keep you in his eyes and guide you in all wisdom and charity."

Kasaf bowed again and watched as Ben Rakasha melted into the crowd.

Chapter 9

The Vineyard Treasure

At the start, a year can seem a long time, but the longer that Ben Rakasha was away, the less Kasaf missed him. Soon it was only every so often that he would stop in his labors as he remembered the teachings of the old man.

But as the year ended, he once again felt the joy of anticipating the return of his beloved master, and on the day in question, he turned the morning sales outside the city completely over to the command of the oldest child in his care, and went early to sit under the tree and await Ben Rakasha.

Yet as he approached the edge of the market hours early, to his surprise the old man was already seated under its shade.

Kasaf approached and bowed deeply while smiling at his master.

"I wonder sometimes," began Kasaf, "when you are always here before me, if you just sit here all day, but I will admit that I have checked, and it was never so."

Ben Rakasha smiled and stood to greet his pupil. "It is good to see you Kasaf and look how you have grown."

"Both in stature and wealth my lord, all because of you."

They both sat and adjusted their clothes before Ben Rakasha spoke. "I hear among the market that much has transpired with you since I left. I think I may be under this tree for some time to hear but a small bit of it."

Kasaf continued smiling. "I would have brought you my gain for the year to show you, my lord, but it has grown too heavy to carry. Instead I have left the large portion of it with several money lenders, so that it might accrue silver without my attention."

"Indeed," responded the old man, "Then I might be here even longer than I thought, to hear all you have done. Truly a man knows that his wealth has reached good portion, when it begins to multiply without the work of its father.

So, make me wait no longer for your tale, I pray you begin."

"Before I start with my tale my lord, I wondered if I might be the one to tell a story this time, for it was one that my father told me. It was because of that story and those things which I learned of you, that I found my magic carpet."

Ben Rakasha leaned over to him. "It seems like it might be time for you and me to switch places under this tree."

Even though it was a joke, Kasaf shook his head, "I meant no disrespect my lord."

Ben Rakasha put his hand on the young man's shoulder. "Kasaf, it was not meant in that way. I am saying I am proud that you now learn on your own, and you may share your insight with me.

If I ever become so old that I cannot learn what is new, then maybe it is time that I pass from this earth. I would love to hear what brought you good fortune."

Kasaf began. "While you were away, I kept my eyes looking for a magic carpet. Each day as I left the city, and each day in the market I looked, but I felt that something covered my eyes from finding it.

My father always told me that everything I needed to succeed was already in my hands. It meant that if I looked at what I had,

I would find I already had the ability to make silver with the things around me.

Then he told me the story of the vineyard treasure. He said that once there was a man who had several lazy sons. He had to go away on business and was quite worried that the grapes would not be properly tended in his field.

So, he called his sons in, and informed them that there was a great treasure in the ground of the vineyard, and he would share it with them if they could find it.

The lads, the very next day, went out onto the land, and began to dig through the soil among the grapes, attempting to uncover the riches of which their father had spoken.

After weeks, they had gone through all of the vineyard, but still had not found anything. They felt they must have missed it, so once again, and more carefully, they dug back across the land, leaving not one weed standing.

It was as they were finishing, that their father returned from his journey. His sons greeted him with their frustrations at finding nothing. The father looked to the vineyard and bade them come with him and he would show them the treasure.

Before them, the vines were filled with great quantities of grapes, better than they had ever been. Here is your treasure, as I promised, their father told them, for the tilled earth had enlivened the vines to produce as never before.

So, the family sold the harvest, and the lazy sons were lazy no more, for the feel of silver in their hands, changed their view of hard work and from that moment on, their silver grew as did their lands."

Kasaf finished and looked at his master. "A good story, with good moral, but I am sure you have heard it before. What you have not heard, is how I and the children in my care have brought this story into the real world.

Are you a walker my lord? If not, I can rent a donkey."

Ben Rakasha laughed, "I shall walk lad. I am old, but I can guarantee no matter how far it is, it shall not kill me."

It was about a mile out of the city that Kasaf turned off the road and bid his master to follow him across the dry ground toward a green field growing in the middle of all of the rocky surrounding.

A line of young date trees stood down the middle, and unlike the surrounding land, this was darkened soil with melons and other vegetables growing beside the small trees.

Kasaf stopped at the edge and let Ben Rakasha survey the crop.

"This all yours, lad?" the old man surmised. "Like the garden of the Lord in the midst of the desert."

"This is my magic carpet, my lord. Soil as was in the first garden at the beginnings of the world, revived from a dead earth. There is not a day goes by that one does not stop and ask me or the children how this feat was attained."

Ben Rakasha bent down and ran the dirt through his fingers. "The soil is replenished; tell me all that you have done, and how you have done it, for this day young Kasaf, you have surpassed even my knowledge."

Kasaf knelt next to him.

"I had hoped you would be impressed good sir. It was my father's story that gave me the idea as I walked from the city. The land out here is dead and dry from being farmed to ashes. It was very much like the dusty carpet.

It dawned on me that a dirty old carpet has little use, but to one who could see, it could change the land. I chose this, as it was a good distance from the road, yet easily accessible, with the least rocks that I could see.

It extends two hundred and forty cubits wide and three hundred and sixty cubits long. Enough, if the soil is good, to support a family and have more for market.

The man who owns it, had purchased it with the potential that the city might grow out this way, but it has been many years, and nothing had changed. I bought it from him for two shekels, and I could tell he thought me insane. That was until lately."

Ashar slowly shook his head, "And now it sits, an oasis amid the desert. How did you fix the land when others could not find it feasible?"

"Ah, that is the trick. They have to pay others to do their work, so they thought it not worth the wage, but the children and I are paid by owning it.

The first thing we did, was to clear all of the rocks and use them to create the borders of the plot.

Then we needed compost and manure to restore its life. Rather than pay for it, I purchased baskets for all of us, and each day as we walked in the city we would scrape up the dung left in the streets by the work animals of the city, plus fruit rinds, and other garbage strewn as people threw it away, anything we could find that would work.

Each morning we would bring it back and work it into a small section at a time, and over two months, we slowly brought the soil back to life. As we did not have the cost of the dung or labor, it raises the profit of the land if we sell.

Not only did it fix the soil, but it gave the children a task, so they could finally be part of helping. It was hard, but it gave them a great sense of self-worth that one cannot achieve without it.

When one comes from a place of feeling worthless, nothing fills that emptiness inside more than creating something worthwhile around you.

After the land was ready, I purchased some young date trees and planted them down the middle, so that the ground could have two crops at separate times."

"All of this is the product of hard work and patience, but even I can tell there is more," added the old man. "Your land is lush as if the rains fall only here. Where is your water source?"

"That is the real magic of what you see." answered Kasaf. "When I first came early the morning after purchase to our new land, my intent was for everyone to simply begin removing the rocks.

As we began, I noticed a large glazed pottery shard left from a broken pot. It was covered with dew that was trickling down the pot and into the ground. Several weeds and some grass grew there, which made me realize that one might use pottery like this to collect dew from the air each night which might water a tree.

I had the children find as many broken glazed pots as they could, that people had thrown away, and we spread them overlapping in a circle where one might plant a tree.

Sure enough, in the morning, the dew had cascaded down the shards and wet the soil at the base with enough water that a date tree will grow with only a little more needed, every day or so.

With that I began buying date trees. We dug holes and filled them with compost, planted the trees, and then laid the pottery about. The trees have doubled in size since we began and in several more years will give fruit."

Ben Rakasha pointed at the base of the fruit vines. "But this is not what you have done next to the melons. What have you done there?"

Kasaf drew back the vine leaves to allow Ben Rakasha to see.

"You will observe I have a pot next to each of the melon roots. The other farmers pour out water on them each day, but I noticed that most of it pours down the mound, and even if it is properly banked, some of the water goes to the roots, but most dries up in the sun.

So, it came to me, that if I watered them more slowly, a trickle at a time, and covered over where the water was, that it would have time to seep into the soil, and I could use less water for the same crop. This would be much like the pot shard trickling a little water all of the time.

I thought about different things, but it came to me that always using the simplest answer to fix a problem was the wisest course of action. It would cost the least, because it would be the simplest.

So, I took a pot and worked a very small hole at the bottom of one edge.   I filled it with water and watched it slowly drip out. I made a small space in the dirt under the pot to catch the water, and it waters slowly all day.

Every ten days, we clean the hole, but other than that, it works. This means we only have to haul half the water that the other farmers do, and because we are not watering anywhere more than that, the weeds do not grow either, meaning less work to keep up the garden. Even the leaves can feed a goat, and the goat produces dung to enrich more earth and milk to sell.

For the future, it means that we can work twice as much land as normal because we have half of the work. The more land I buy, the more children without homes we can feed and train to be farmers with land that they may own. The city will have more food, and everyone benefits."

Ben Rakasha stood and smelled the fresh melons and green amid the dry hot air. "This, young Kasaf, is truly a marvel to behold. Your crop shall pay for more land, your farming practices will bring about great change and much more food, and it shall also help many to learn a trade."

"Yes," added Kasaf, "and it is also my third basket, so not all of my feathered offspring are together. Already I have been offered ten times what I paid for the land."

"I am away twelve moons and you have discovered marvels that others have not in hundreds of years. I can only imagine what shall occur in your lifetime. Truly my young Kasaf, you bring honor to my belief in you."

"It honors me that you say so my lord, you have raised, and treated, me as a father would his only son; it is the least I can do to return your trust in me. Should you ask, all of this is yours, for without you I would have none of it."

Ben Rakasha smiled, "My heart is full, with your success Kasaf, and my needs have long since been supplied. There is nothing more that keeps me to this earth, than to watch how you succeed. Now come, let us walk the city and you can show me what has changed in my absence."

Chapter 10

The Raven and the Pitcher

As they walked through the city, Ben Rakasha noticed an old merchant at the edge of the market. "Can you see the sadness on the face of Ben Tharakha, the old potter?" he asked.

Kasaf nodded, "I have seen him so for many days; what troubles him so?"

"His only son took ill shortly after the last moon and passed on thereafter. This is what has stolen his life, and his stall empties each day, as he no longer sees the point to make new items to sell.

It is a great tragedy for a man to have to bury his children before him. Add to that, he has no one to pass his trade unto, and now he is too poor to care for himself in the years to come.

Now I am afraid, Kasaf, that his future holds little but to beg at the gate in his old age.”

Kasaf looked at the old merchant and then back at his master.

“You point this out for a purpose my lord, for you have the wealth to ease this sufferance, yet you direct me forth.”

Ben Rakasha smiled, “Am I that obvious young Kasaf? I must learn to hint more softly toward you.”

Kasaf watched the old potter. “Then my lord, here I have not a problem, but an answer that as of yet I do not see. You show me a potter with no heir, and no one to continue his craft. Before me there must lie silver for both he and I so that it may benefit both. All I have to do is see it.

I have no time to work the market for him, and I cannot bring one of the children to learn of his trade, for he has not the years left to train, and they would be too young to run his craft”.

Ben Rakasha nodded, “Perhaps a story will help?”

Kasaf smiled, “Then back to the tree it is, my lord.”

It was but minutes later that they once again sat down under the familiar shade by the market, and Ben Rakasha readied himself to begin.

"I was going to tell a simple tale," winked Ashar, "but I believe I shall spin a harder one to see how keen your mind has become.

There once was a raven, who upon a very hot day, such as this, noticed a tall, old glazed pitcher with a wide brim sitting upon the ground.

Curious, the raven looked inside and saw water at the bottom, for each night, dew would collect on the brim of the pitcher and drip inside. As the pitcher was deep, the raven could not easily put his head inside and drink from the water.

Here then lay the problem. The raven knew if he could find a way to get to the water, it would be there each day, if only he could find a way to reach it.

As he could not bring himself to the water, he knew he had to bring the water to him.

He had an idea. He went along the road, and began to pick up very small pebbles, placing them one at a time into the pitcher.

The level of the water began to rise, and after many pebbles were placed in the pitcher, the water was high enough for the raven to drink. Now, as long as the pitcher stood, the raven knew he would always have water."

Ben Rakasha finished and looked at Kasaf.

"Do the eyes of wisdom speak to you, regarding my tale."

Kasaf smiled, "That one is harder than your others, but I am older now and it is as it should be to challenge my thoughts."

It is simple to understand that I am the raven, as I must be the one who is to collect the pebbles to put into the pitcher that is empty except for a little water.

That means that the pitcher is not just the potter, but the stall in the market where he works, for I cannot stick physical items into a man. The pitcher is old, and so are both the potter and his booth, for he has been here many years.

He is empty, and his booth lacks the fullness it needs, for the loss of his son has destroyed both his future and his heart, so there is little left in either him or his booth.

If I am the raven, then I need to find pebbles along the road that may be put in the booth to bring up the water. The water is that which the raven needs to live, so it might symbolize what profit the booth may produce.

If I fill it with the right pebbles, the potter will then be full once again, and I also may draw from the booth each day. The only question that remains, is what are the pebbles that I must place with him."

Ben Rakasha nodded, "Excellent. you grasp the meaning as quickly as you had the first things that I shared with you. Now the only puzzle you have to unravel, as you have said, is the meanings of the pebbles."

"I noticed that you said along the road. You never have added anything to the stories that did not have meaning, so I also need to understand the road."

"And why are you the raven?"

"That was not lost on me. The raven is black, and I as a homeless child was as black as this raven, yet my mind was still sharp. Ravens look for items they might scavenge, but they are also traders. They collect shiny items of beauty and will trade them for food or other things of value to them.

I, in this same way, have collected silver in abundance by trading items of value. The last thing, is that the raven with time and thought, was able to solve this problem both to the benefit of the pitcher and himself."

"Very good."

"So, if this story directly shadows me, then I shall find the pebbles at the road. The road I go to, is the one which the caravans travel. So, I might surmise that something of the caravans are the pebbles spoken of."

"Also good."

Kasaf sighed. "If I may request, may I have two days to see what answer I may find."

Ben Rakasha nodded in agreement and stood. In two days, young man, I shall return, and we shall see if the Raven can fill the pitcher and give drink to those in need."

Kasaf bowed and sat down and looked back to wave, but oddly his master had already disappeared among those in the market.

Chapter 11

The Chariot Maker's Wife

For Kasaf, it was a hectic two days, attempting to find a solution for his problem. When he finally met Ben Rakasha under the tree, he was noticeably worn.

He sat down next to his master and let out a deep sigh.

The old man looked him over. "I'm so sorry Kasaf. Next time maybe I should give you a week. There is no failure in taking more time for an endeavor. If at first attempt it does not succeed, then recoup, learn from what did not give success and begin again.

I appreciate your zeal to impress me young man, but I also want you to be strong enough to continue in your day. You will not fail me by taking longer. Sometimes, that is the success.

Remember that a well that only empties, soon has no value. Take one day each week to rest. During this time, enjoy the things which you have created and have been given. Spend time with those you care for, and also care for yourself.

It is days like that, which give you time to back away from the race you run and allows you to see if your course needs correction.

It is those days where you will most see the silver appear above your head, that would be missed in the hustle of the workday."

Kasaf nodded in understanding.

Ben Rakasha continued. "That having been said, you walked not as one weighted with failure, so please tell me of your solution."

Kasaf took a deep breath and faced Ashar.

"My frustration was the pebbles of the road my lord. I pondered this for the better part of a day. I then realized I was again over thinking the solution. If the potter's booth was empty, what was it empty of?

Pottery of course.

I felt much the fool to have missed an answer such that a child would have seen it, but armed with the idea, I inquired the next day of the caravans and their wares of pots and the like.

There was a good selection of everything from decorative to work pieces. All finished and ready to sell to the merchants.

I needed not to have one learn the potters craft; I needed only to drop pebbles into his booth to fill it.

With this, I approached Ben Tharakha and explained to him my plan. I wished to slowly begin to stock my wares amid his booth. We would then share in the profits, the larger portion going to him.

When he could no longer work, I would assume the booth, and continue to pay him a portion of the profits as payment for his name and his area in the market until the day he shall pass."

He has agreed to this, and tomorrow he and I shall see an elder and a scribe to seal our contract.

Even today, without yet putting a pebble in his store, the water has begun to rise, for he has once again busied himself to make pots and pitchers that might hang at his booth."

Ashar smiled, "Such a simple answer to so many problems, was it not young Kasaf? Now we have a man with hope, you have a share in the market, and your silver only increases."

"Yes, my lord, and more than that, I have observed the industrious women of the city who make pots and such at their homes with their hands instead of the potters' wheel.

It came to me, that they might make such items and I could sell them, that they might create copper for themselves when they had time.

With just this one booth, I can have wealth flow to many families instead of just one and have my prosperity spread to others."

"And this is how any good endeavor should be planned. If one is wise, many may benefit. As a single stone dropped in the pond, its ripples may be felt shore to shore and back again.

Now, let us speak of Tharakha. As you said, his spirits have lifted, and once again he has his hands to the wheel. So, tell me, why is this so?

You have not placed new pottery to his shop, you have not signed with the scribe. His son has still passed on. Nothing has yet changed, and yet he is enlivened. How do you account for it?

"I assume that it is because he has a future, my lord?"

"Let me tell you a story Kasaf.

There once was a chariot maker, who made fine chariots, but never made great amounts of money. Even so, over the years he had put aside a good amount of silver for when his hands could ply their trade no more.

One day, the king's man approached, for he had heard of the builder's skill. He looked over his work and asked him to build one for the captain of the army. If it was well crafted and pleased the captain, they would order many more.

The chariot builder was filled with excitement and rushed home to tell his wife. When he entered the house, he found her in tears.

The children had worn her down all day. The pen had been left open and the chickens had escaped and to finish it all, while she was out chasing them, the goat entered the house and ate the bread for he evening meal that she had left to cool.

The chariot builder was so saddened by her plight, that he drew out his savings, placed them in the hand of his wife and bid her buy those things that she had desired through the years.

The wife immediately jumped up, filled with joy, and as she ran to change her attire to go to the market. The chariot maker who was over joyed to share his news, found himself sink to sadness with the loss of his hard earned savings."

Ben Rakasha finished.

"Now tell me Kasaf, how is it that nothing has changed except how both felt? The sobbing wife had not yet purchased, yet she was now elated. The money had not left his house, yet the overjoyed chariot maker was now saddened."

"I suppose my lord it is because they look at what is to come, and no longer at what is."

"Exactly! Just like Tharakha. The loss of his son, and what he saw for his future, weighed heavy on him. Based on what he *thought* his future held, he chose to lose all hope, and thus, chose to cease his labor, thus self fulfilling his fear.

Yet none of that future was real. Your offer has changed death unto life. Even though you have, as yet, done nothing, the water of his pitcher has begun to fill."

Kasaf thought. "So, what you are saying, is that it is our choice how we feel no matter the situation, for we know not the future. If we choose to "feel" our way through life based on our beliefs of what is to come, we shall be like a ship on a stormy sea, blown here and there as the wind chooses."

"Very much," replied Ben Rakasha. "You are the captain of your ship. It is your hand on the rudder. As we have no real knowledge of tomorrow, then why not live full of expectation of success no matter what might come. For the one filled thus, is full of power, and may put their hand to their craft with all their might."

"It is as you said to me, a long time ago, that our feelings are a great slave, but a terrible task master."

"Yes. Master them, and make them work for you, and they shall put silver, both in your purse and in the hearts of those around you, or let them run free and watch your silver take flight."

Kasaf nodded. "This I have come to understand. Things may occur that shall set a mountain before your path. Do not use them as an excuse to turn back, but as a reason to learn to climb.

 Every problem is simply an answer you would not have looked for, without it.

If one understands this, then every problem that besets itself before you, should be met with excitement, for riches lay in discovering its answer."

"Yes, young Kasaf. And they shall find the answer with much more speed for their heart remains high.

Now with that my young man, you need naught more from me. By your hand and wisdom, I bid you continue on this journey.

My path calls me away again, for another twelve moons, but it is a journey that shall end with riches few could imagine. This will touch the lives of everyone in this city and to the ends of the land itself."

Kasaf tried not to look saddened at the news.

Ashar smiled, "Good try my young Kasaf, keep practicing and soon that smile will reside in your heart and on your face.

Now be of cheer, for great adventure lays before you in the coming time. Be here again on this day in twelve moons, and on that day, you shall see a wonder unlike anything this city has ever seen."

Ben Rakasha clasped his hands to Kasaf's and they bowed together before the old man turned and was, a usual, lost in the milling of the market.

Chapter 12

The Masters Ring

Twelve moons had passed to the day, and for the first time in all of their meetings, Kasaf was first to the tree in the market. An hour went by, and he began to wonder if he had come on the wrong day, when his master appeared at the edge of the crowd and made his way to him.

The old man bowed deeper than he ever had, before Kasaf, and then sat down next to the young man.

"It does my eyes and my heart great happiness to see you one more time my son. Great has been your year and my ears tickle to hear your stories."

Kasaf stood and bowed to the ground before the old man. "To him who has been as a father to me, who's wisdom has lifted me from the pit to the throne of a king, may the hand of your maker never cease from finding you shelter."

Ben Rakasha stood and placed his hands on Kasaf's shoulders. "Rise, my son, and show me the work of your hand."

Kasaf stood, and he and Ashar walked through the market. In the twelve moons, Kasaf had acquired not one, but four booths in the market, each diverse of the other, each overflowing with goods and those who might purchase.

He had trained the young people under him well, and they learned to run each of the booths, well versed in the trade and the barter.

He then took him outside of the city gates, where he saw the elders acknowledge young Kasaf as they passed, for his name and the wisdom of his ways had gained a name for him even at the gates of the city. Never had one so young done so much.

Outside of the gates, they had no need to walk far as they had a year before, for now a great area around was as Kasaf's small plot.

"How is this so?" asked Ben Rakasha.

"All of this is my land, but I have taught those who wished land, the workings of mine, and they, as I, have been able to raise gardens. Even the king himself has come to see what we have done and given money forth that a well was dug here, that we might increase turning back the soil to profitable land.”

Ben Rakasha marveled at what lay before him. Young date trees lined the road out from the gate, giving way to lush growth on each side for a mile out from the city gates. He shook his head in wonder.

“Never, my son, has there been one such as you, for never has one so young, never mind an old man such as myself, worked such wonders in so little time.

Truly there is no one as rich as you, for your wealth does not lie merely in silver, but in wisdom and creation and the teaching of wisdom and charity to those around.

This only affirms what I need next of you, and I am sorry that I have not much time to once again spend with you. I have one more task that I need of you that is of great importance, for I am readied to begin a long journey and I shall not see you again for many years.”

Kasaf smiled, this time he was able to do it both with his heart and his face. “I somehow knew that my time with you would be short this time my father. I assume this task has something to do with what you spoke of before you left last time.”

Ben Rakasha nodded.

"This task is but a short road that will lead to a longer one that will bring great hope to the city and the land, but before I tell you what I need, let me tell you one more story as we walk.

Back when we first met, I told you the story of Alladan and the three scrolls, but I never told you how he was released from the cave, for that at the time was not what mattered. But now I will finish that tale, as it now shall allow you to begin a new journey to add to your own.

Allahdan sat among the darkness of the cave and wondered what might become of him. When his eyes adjusted to the dim light, he noticed a soft glow in front of him.

Reaching down, he found a ring with a single gem which glowed softy in the shallow light of the room. At the edge of the cave, another glow along the wall also caught his attention. He carefully walked over the jewels and other treasures at his feet, to the glow coming from a small square with an impression in the middle.

The inscription in the panel read; *those who wield the masters signet shall safely pass.* Allahdan looked down at the ring and the indentation in the wall and realized they matched. He placed the ring into it and pushed but to no avail.

Again, but this time he turned the ring, and with a click, the panel popped open.   Inside was a lever, which Allahdan pulled, and in an instant, the wall of the cave next to the panel slid slowly to the side as a great weight pulled the rock away.

Inside, Allahdan saw a dim light and stairs, which he climbed until he reached the top and another open door. As he stepped out into the night air unto the stone at the mouth of the entrance, it sank down, and with a rumble, the doors behind him slid shut to be unnoticed once more.

Outside on the wall, he noticed the same impression that matched the one in the cave. Allahdan realized that the ring held the key to all of the riches of a kingdom, and with them, he became the wealthiest man in the kingdom with all of his wishes granted."

Ben Rakasha finished and looked at Kasaf.

"This story is not for you to figure now. I want you to hold it, and soon you will use it as Allahdan did, to unlock the greatest treasure in the land."

"Is this what you spoke about before, that you were to tell me when you returned?"

"Yes. Now here is the last task I need from you. I wish you to go to my home; you know where it is. Tell them you have a message from me that you must convey. Tell them you have been commanded to speak these words that I give you to no one except the sister of Ben Rakasha.

When my sister meets you, she shall test you. What you hear, you will not believe. Stay firm in what you know and when you do, the tale of Allahdan will give you the answer.

Do you understand what I ask?"

Kasaf looked his master in the eyes, "I need not understand my lord, I need only to obey as you have commanded me."

Ben Rakasha whispered words for his sister in his ear and then placed his right hand upon Kasaf's head.

"May you who have been a greater honor than a thousand sons, find your place of honor at the head of the table. May you be guided in all wisdom and with good charity to those beneath you, and a wellspring of knowledge to those who seek it."

Tears welled up in Kasaf's eyes. "I shall not see you again shall I father?"

Asher smiled, "Not for many a day my son, but stay of good heart, you shall in time."

Ben Rakasha clasped Kasaf's hand, and then pulled him toward him and hugged him as his own.

"Good journey my son,"

Kasaf tried to smile, "Good journey my father."

Ben Rakasha bowed and turned but this time not into the market. Instead he walked toward the city gate until Kasaf lost him among the throng of people at its mouth.

When he could see him no more, Kasaf walked the city to come upon the great home of his master.

At the gate, he was met by a servant who asked of his intent. Kasaf told him, and the servant called from the gate to another closer to the house.

The second servant opened the gate and bid him follow. At the door, he knocked twice, then waited, then knocked again. The door opened to another of the house, who spoke with the servant and then looked oddly at Kasaf.

"Hold up your arms and extend your hands," the servant demanded.

They checked for any weapons, and realizing there were none, bade the young man to follow. He was led to a large room with chairs and a table, behind which were many scrolls stacked among shelves in the wall. The walls were painted with scenes from the very stories that Ashar had shared with him.

As he was noting them, a door on the other wall of the room opened and the same servant and an old woman entered. She approached the table and bid Kasaf to sit.

"I am told," she began, that you have a message from my brother."

"Yes," replied Kasaf, "he said I was to speak it to you and no other."

"Then speak it young man," she replied.

"He bade me tell you that the gem he has searched for stands before you."

The old woman frowned, "And just when did my brother give you this message?"

"Today mistress, at the tree by the market edge."

She looked angry. "You lie. Why are you here?"

"I do not lie mistress, he bid me come and speak with you!"

The old woman looked coldly at Kasaf. "Tell me young man, how does my brother speak with you, as he passed from this world years ago!"

Kasaf looked bewildered, "That is not possible, for years my master Ben Rakasha has taught me of his wisdom, that I might rise from the streets to great wealth."

The sister frowned again. "And what be your name, he who spins tales of a youth of self-made riches?"

"I am Kasaf, the one who has restored the land at the cities gates."

The woman frowned again and exchanged whispers with her servant. They finished and she once again turned to him. "Your name precedes you, Kasaf, but your gain does not change the lie that you speak. My brother requested that his passing go without report, so none of the city know. Why do you sit here and mock his name?!"

Kasaf swallowed hard, "I should never mock my great master's name. He sent me here to speak these words to you. If you do not believe me, then test me as he foretold you would do.

The old woman looked to her servant, then to the wall and then back to Kasaf. "If my brother spoke with you, tell me the story of the magic lamp."

Kasaf brightened, "It was not a lamp mistress, but three scrolls. They were riddles he spoke to me. I solved them and used them to increase my silver."

Kasaf's attention was drawn past the old woman to the wall.

"The scrolls looked just like the three on the shelf behind you, the brown ones together."

The old woman turned and looked at the wall and then back to Kasaf. "You could not know that!"

"I can," replied Kasaf, "and I can tell you what they say and what they mean!"

The old woman bade her servant to retrieve the scrolls and unroll them on the table. She looked upon the words of the first one and then to Kasaf. "Speak!"

Kasaf closed his eyes and saw the scroll, as if it was the first day he had opened them.

"It says silver must have three, and there are three things listed below. These things must be done to have silver.

The mouth of a beggar means one should always give to those who cannot work. So, if you have one hundred coins, ten should go to those in need.

Eighty for the workman, those who worked for the silver, so eighty out of every one hundred the worker should keep for himself."

And the last, ten silvers out of every one hundred, pay for seed that would be sowed.

It means that you should set aside that ten to invest. If you use it to buy things right away, it would be like eating your seed, but if you sow it properly, like a crop, more silver will grow."

The woman's face grew ashen as Kasaf spoke and the servant moved to steady her, but she stopped him and asserted herself.

"This is not possible; it cannot be my brother who taught these things to you. There could be duplicates that others have; I know not where he even came into ownership of them."

Kasaf didn't understand, but he continued.

"One more time I repeat, for the last years, Ben Rakasha has cared for the needs of me and other children of the street, and in that time taught me such that my wealth is beyond any of my age. I need not of your house; I am only here to speak, as I have been commanded, and leave."

He told me that his journey shall end with riches few could imagine, that will touch the lives of everyone in this city and to the ends of the land itself."

Ben Rakasha's sister stopped. "Say that again."

"His journey shall end with riches few could imagine, that will touch the lives of everyone in this city."

The old woman sat down and bid her servant to leave.

"My brother's wealth, when he was alive, was so great that it could not be counted by the scribes. Some say it was greater than the king himself. When my brother was young, he was no different than any of us, until one day the old prophet Jeremiah, the captive prophet of Israel spoke over him.

Understand that we are the Judeans, who were brought here many years ago when Israel fell to the old Babylonian king.

As I said, my brother was as every other, until Jeremiah spoke to him, and then everything changed. It was as if the wisdom of the sages had descended upon him, and within years, he had amassed wealth beyond imagination, much like you have begun.

Then, just before his death, without my knowledge, all of it was sold and turned into silver and disappeared from the face of the earth.

All he told me was that my needs and those of the household were taken care of, but the rest would remain hidden to touch the lives of everyone in this city and our people when the silver spoke to me. You could not have known those words unless you had spoken with him. How is this possible?"

Kasaf sat in the chair, unsure of what to say. His eyes wandered the room, as his mind tried to understand the possibilities of what his master's sister had said.

Then quietly he spoke. "For the last several years, your brother would come and sit with me under the tree at the edge of the market. He would tell me stories and through those fables, teach me the secrets of wealth, which I followed with all heart.

Now as I sit here, you tell me that my master was not of this earth. That from beyond this world he searched for me and trained me and bid me to be here.

He would not have done this without purpose. He also said that once I was here, that the story of how Allahdan escaped from the cave would then make sense to me.

The old woman looked up, "He would never tell anyone the ending of that story. Why would he speak it to you?"

Kasaf stood from the chair, "He told me it was just for this moment."

Slowly he turned behind him, to follow the paintings on the wall. Each a scene from the stories Ben Rakasha had told him.

There at the back, Allahdan knelt among the treasures with the ring in his hand.

Kasaf reach to his chest and drew up a chain with Ben Rakasha's ring at the end of it.

"What is it?" asked the old woman.

"It is the ring my master gave me at the beginning. He said it was his ring, and now I understand."

Kasaf walked to the painting, examined the ring in his hand, a perfect match to the artwork. His eyes followed along until he saw the panel on the cave wall in the story. His fingers traced it and he could feel the indent. Placing the face of the ring in, he turned it and the panel popped open.

Kasaf turned and looked at Ben Rakasha's sister. She arose and hurried to the wall. As in the tale, the lever lay there waiting to be pulled. Kasaf reached in and turned it until it clicked, and a rumbling began as if a great weight moved.

The painting cracked in the middle and the wall drew back to reveal a massive chamber filled with bars of silver and vats of shekels and items of great value stacked as high as one stands, throughout the room.

The old woman put her hand to her mouth as she stared at what lay before them. On a small table at the entrance to the room lay a single scroll.

The old woman unrolled it and read it to herself and then looked up at Kasaf. "Your name in Hebrew, young man, means silver in my tongue."

Kasaf nodded, "I have been told this."

"Then this day, silver has spoken to me. Let me read this to you; *To whose eyes first come upon this scroll, let it be known, that I Ashar Ben Rakasha commands that when silver comes to this room and speaks, and, by his hand and my ring, this treasure is found, then this shall come to be:*

This great treasure is set aside to be used for the betterment of the Judean people and the peoples of this city by the hand of he who reveals it. For this was foretold to me by the Prophet Jeremiah in my youth, and as it has been spoken, and as it has come to pass, let it be so.

Kasaf looked horrified, "I do not understand."

Ben Rakasha's sister looked up with tears in her eyes. "My brother has spoken with you and trained you up. All of these years, he never wavered, looking for the gem that the prophet told him he would find and train. Even when he passed into the hands of our maker, he kept upon that path.

You, young man, have shown yourself refined in your path, and it has been foretold that you shall now be in charge of all that was his, to do as he knew you would. To change the lives of the peoples of this city."

Kasaf shook his head, "But I am just a boy, not an elder, I cannot do these things!"

The old woman smiled and put her hands on his shoulders. "From what I have heard, young Kasaf, you already have been. Now you just have the tools to do more in my brother's name."

Kasaf looked at the treasure in the room and then back into the eyes of the old woman.

"Then, as my master has bid me," whispered Kasaf, "It shall be done."

Epilogue

In the years that followed, Ben Rakasha's wealth was used wisely by Kasaf and he changed the lives of those in the city and the land. Through his hand, the people of the city prospered and created many things of such wonder that it drew merchants and travelers from all over the world to see them.

He lived a long life, married well, and had many children, all who grew in the wisdom of their father until the day they and the people of Israel returned at the command of king Cyrus, to their former land.

Some think that riches are merely silver, but the people came to know that it was not the coin in one's hand that gave riches, but what is created with it and for whom. These are the things that become stored in your heart and these are the things that make people as stars.

Go forth and do the same.

The Four Silvers

The Ideas of Man

The Owning of Land

The Storing of Food

The Waste of Want

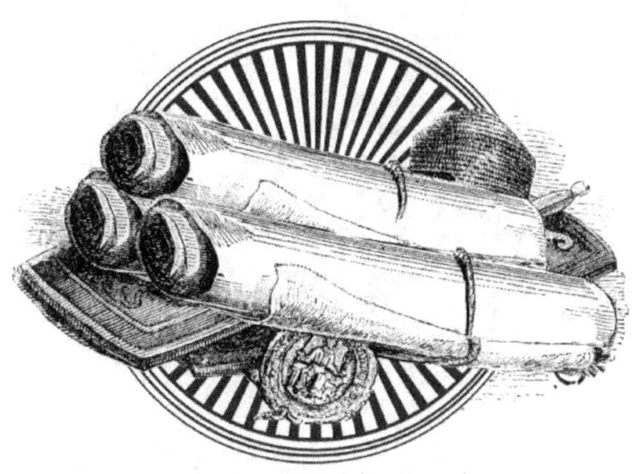

The First Scroll

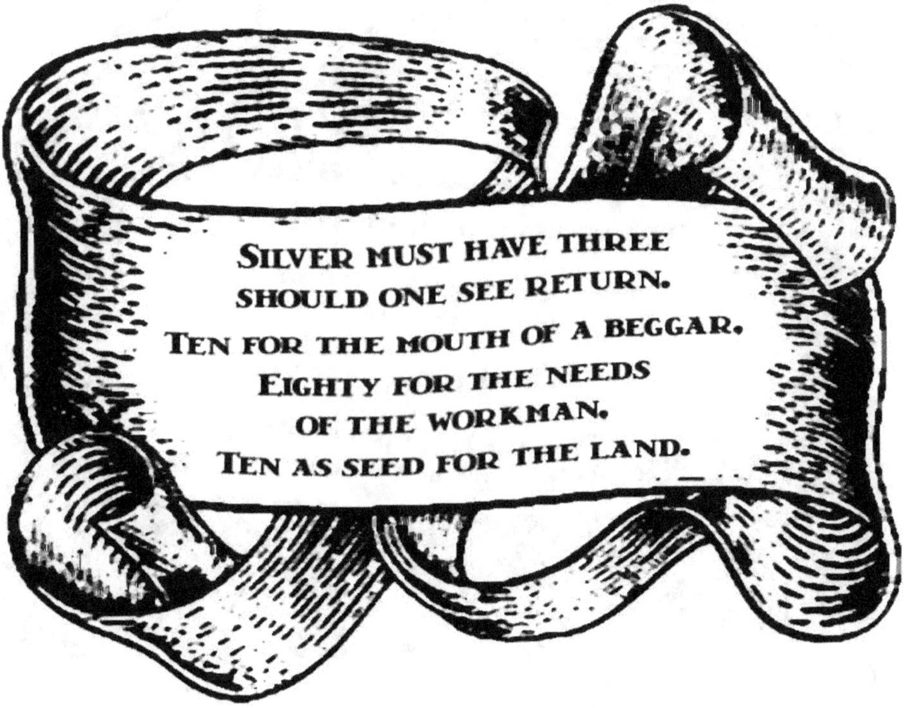

The Second Scroll

The Third Scroll

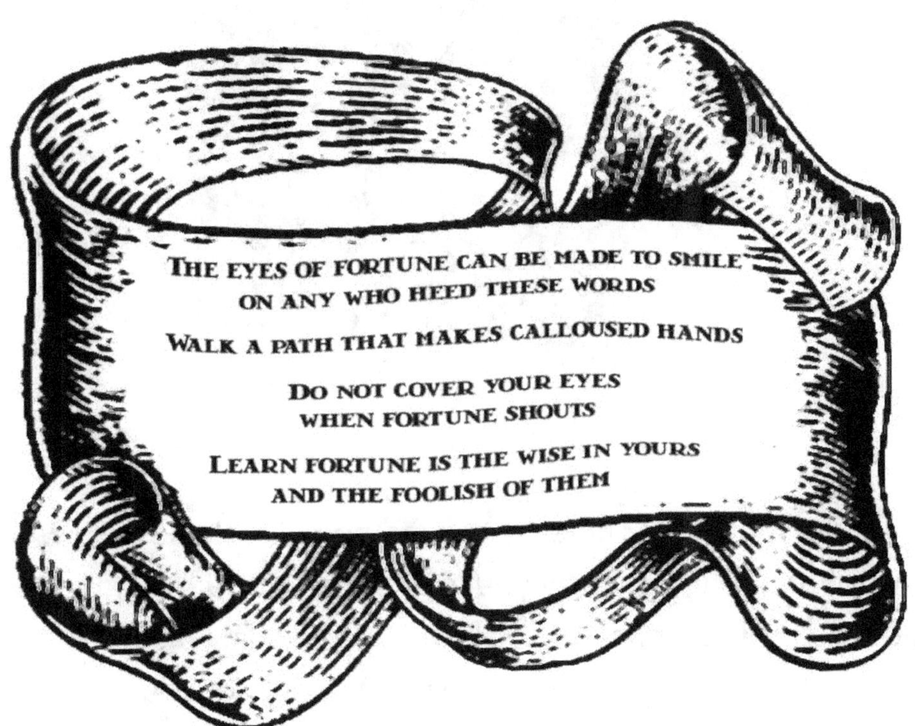

Also, by this author

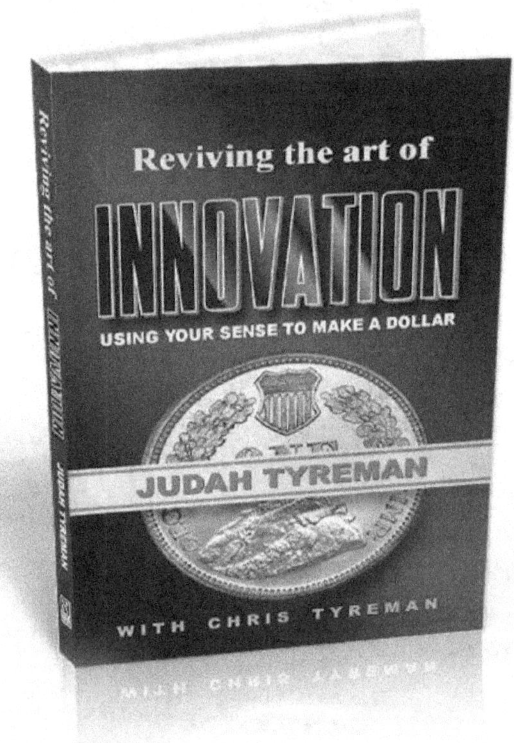

If you're looking for an easy to read book for those 8-80 which will change the very way you look at the world, and give your kids the tools to innovate, and create personal wealth from the get go, this is the must have book for you.

Here is the first chapter from "Reviving the Art of Innovation"

Chapter 1

Tikkun Olam

What do I know?

My name is Judah Tyreman and at the time of this writing I am a 15 years old, tall skinny Jewish kid with pimple problems and dyslexia living in a really small Canadian town.

So, I am just like you.

Except I'm not.

The difference is that I don't believe the things you believe. I don't believe that I have to wait around until I'm eighteen before I can start something amazing.

I don't believe the impossible is impossible.

I don't believe that I need to go to school for twelve years, and then to University where I could accrue a loan debt of $80,000.00 (if I was lucky) that I could spend the next ten to twenty years paying off before I started building my personal wealth.

Instead I went a different route. With my parents' help, I schooled myself, mowed lawns until there was no sweat left in my pores and slowly collected rocks and gems until I had enough to start a full-time company with my hobby.

In doing so, I became the youngest museum curator in the world by opening the Sesula Mineral & Gem Museum located in my really small town of Radisson, Saskatchewan Canada.

A Museum? That's so lame!

It sure is, and my net worth this year is way over $150,000.00 and on top of that, in the last four years I have given away over $20,000 to charities and people in need.

The impossible is only impossible until it's not.

Not so lame now is it?

I have appeared on television, and radio programs, all over North America, including the Discovery Channel, and a four page spread in the best mineral magazine in the world; Rock and Gem Magazine International.

I also received top honors in the 2018 Get a Bigger Wagon Young Entrepreneur Awards at the Edwards School of Business, at the University of Saskatchewan. The Haddocks, who sponsored this award, presented me with $1000.00 in cold, hard cash, for placing first in the 13 to 15-year-old category.

Bragging? No. I have a point to all this.

If a guy just like you, living in a small town of five hundred, with no bank loan and a simple idea can do this, then I can teach all of you to do the same.

That's why I wrote this book, because what I did was not accidental, but planned.

I'm using the same method to create this book, that I used to create my business, and I'm going to show you how you can make your ideas a reality also, whether you are eight or eighty.

Do I guarantee your positive success? No, but I can guarantee that you will have the base tools you need to do it.

**I can only show you the door,
you have to walk through it.**
-Morpheus-

So, before we get into that, let me tell you what my idea was which made the Sesula museum so unique.

The museum is not just any museum, this is a one of a kind. The Sesula Mineral & Gem Museum is the only hands on mineral and gem museum in North America. I have people stop in from all over the world, who have seen me on television, heard me on radio, or were told about me through word of mouth.

That having been said, I didn't set out to build another museum, I set out to think like an innovator.

An innovator is something that people mistakenly call an entrepreneur.

An entrepreneur is usually someone who starts a business. An innovator is someone who sees problems and finds ways to fix them.

So not all innovators are entrepreneurs, but all successful entrepreneurs are innovators.

I didn't just set out to build a museum. I set out to build something that had never been done before. I took an old idea, and made it new, made it better.

This is one of the easiest ways to come up with a new idea; take something that has already been done and do it better.

How?

Fix the problems with the old idea.

**Fix a problem that everyone has
And they will beat a path to your door.**

You don't need a new idea to create a company or make money. You don't need to come up with the latest internet craze or be some computer whiz to be the next millionaire kid. You just need to learn a different way of looking at what is already there.

Make it faster or slower, make it more fun or easier, cheaper or more expensive, but fix the problems with the old idea. Simply create the solution that people want by doing it in a way that's new.

This is what I set out to do.

But first, for you, I need to answer the question; why a museum.

The museum is named after a friend of mine, Stewart Sesula, who I met while looking for new mineral samples for a summer display I was involved in when I was ten.

Stewart was a quadriplegic, which is a real game changer in a person's life. It happened to Mr. Sesula when he was young, and when most people would just give up on life. He didn't focus on what he didn't have but on what he could do with what he had. So, he began buying and selling minerals.

Over the summer, as donations came in on the display I had, I used it to buy new pieces from Mr. Sesula. At the end of the summer, he came out to see the display which had grown to fill eight hundred square feet.

He told me he was really impressed, and I felt good about that, knowing his knowledge of my collection.

Then, Stewart caught double pneumonia, and passed away so quickly, that I didn't have time to say goodbye. Later, I received a call, that Mr. Sesula had left some of his collection to me, asking if I could use it with mine to do something with it for kids.

Stewart knew that one of my motivations in doing displays, was to put people back in touch with the real world, and off of their tech devices. So much so, that the slogan of the museum is still…

"Welcome to the real world."

It was because of that request, and the enjoyment of the success of the four-month summer display, that after discussing it with my family, I decided to open a museum in his honor.

Nice idea, but I was not comfortable with the present idea of a museum.

Why?

Everything is either "DO NOT TOUCH" or behind glass and as a kid on the net, I can see anything in that form on a Youtube video.

This is a new world, and the old idea of a museum needs to change in order to bring in a younger audience.

Knowing this, if I wanted people to see what we have, I needed something no one had tried before. So, if you are thinking of trying something new, there is a path that you need to learn so you don't waste valuable time learning from your mistakes.

**You learn most from mistakes,
try not to let them be yours**

So, the first thing, was to analyze everything I disliked about museums and innovate a way of fixing them, and also incorporate what I learned from my summer display.

Don't get me wrong, I love museums, but ideas can be improved.

The largest problem I saw

Most museums suffer from one or more problems.   What I noticed was…
1. Either they charge you to enter or...
2. Rely on donations or...
3. Both.

I knew there had to be a better way, and this is where thinking like an innovator comes in.

I needed to fix these problems:
1. A museum that relies on donation is continually fighting to find enough monies and...

2. A charge shuts out the people that have low incomes and that keeps kids and big families away.

____

People should never be stopped from learning because they are poor.

____

The third problem with museums is more unique to my generation:

3. As I said before, why go to look at something behind glass when I can watch it on Youtube and still be looking through glass.

So, if I wanted kids and adults to come, I had to:

- make the glass disappear
- and the entrance fee,
- and the need for relying solely on donation to support the venture.

Here is how I did it.

Answer one: no more glass

All of the displays are hands on, which is probably the thing which weirds parents out the most when they come in.

Everyone can touch and pick up everything from minerals to meteorites, from jewels to dinosaur bones.

The difference is obvious in their reaction. Watching for the first time when you see a kid feel a real dino femur, the weight alone changes how they now see the item, and that moment sticks with them for the rest of their lives.

**We live now in a fake world that no one believes in anymore.
It's time to come back to the real world**

Does it have problems? Sure, some of the samples need to be washed from time to time. There is more dusting, and there was that one three-year-old that hucked that rock he picked up straight at a glass window, which rang like a bell.

(I thought the mom was going to die of a heart attack, but the window was fine).

Answer two: have the displays fund the museum

In most museums there is a gift shop. It's a separate store full of nothing you saw at the museum. Sure, there is some cool stuff in there, but what's the point?

You get all excited about things you saw in the museum, but you can't take any of it home, so that excitement doesn't stay with you and you forget what you learned and go back to building calluses on your thumbs playing with your tech device.

This is not an effective strategy.

When I go to a museum and see something fantastic, that's what I want to take home.

This really hit home to me when I had my summer display and people would stop in and be really disappointed when there was nothing to buy. So, beside many of our museum's displays you can buy samples of the minerals, gems and fossils you see.

In essence, I took the gift shop and spread it throughout the museum.

Next, I priced everything at kid prices so kids of all ages can afford to shop. I don't make huge profit right up front, but I let kids begin to build a collection.

That's what builds a lifelong love of minerals and gems, the ability to collect, so in the long run I build up an ever-increasing return clientele.

I'm kind of the McDonalds of the rock and gem shops.

Sell a lot with a little profit. It takes longer to grow, but you build a stronger customer base.

And for those who don't wish to buy, I still have a donation jar by the entrance in case they wish to help out that way, and they do.

These purchases and donations pay for the museum costs and for expansion so that we are not always trying to find funding. Problem solved.

I could have stopped there, but I need to tell you of a third aspect regarding the museum that is the most important. Museums and other institutions like them have what I call an implosive perspective. They operate waiting for donations, and the way that non-profits are set up, they do not have a choice.

The problem with that is that it sets up the mental perspective that you are a beggar waiting for the generosity of others.

I do not say this to belittle these great institutions, as their hands are tied for how they seek funds, but it sets up a way of thinking that is the opposite of innovation. They have to wait for funds from others, rather than being able to create their own.

This perspective can slowly grind the progress of a charity to snail's pace, and greatly impede its purpose.

So aside from changing the perspective of how our funds are created, I actually have it set up to do the very opposite that a non-profit does. As an innovative business I have that freedom not just to make a profit to use for expansion, but much more.

Any good business has to go beyond just making a profit; it has to give back to the world it exists in.

So we do two things.

1. We give a free mineral sample to every kid who comes through the door, and it changes so it won't always be the same one. This means that no kid leaves the museum without something to remember it by, no matter how poor they are.

You can live your life as a black hole that eats everything that crosses its path, or like a sun that gives out to everything around.   The choice is yours.

Yes, that costs us money, and we don't give out crappy stuff, but cool stuff like Ruby Anyolite from Kenya that has real rubies in it, or Labradorite from Madagascar.

A waste of money? It's the opposite.

What I found was that those gifts bought us amazing good will and word of mouth that wouldn't have occurred without it.

People were so pleased about the free gifts, that they would tell a lot of people about their visit and how to find us. They would even go on the net and post pictures and tell everyone about their tour.

That small gift, returned a fortune in free advertising even though that was not my intent.

2. We donate 10% of all of our sales to support people in need. We donate to everything from families in our area that need food, to across the world with a Christian orphanage in Africa.

We, the Jewish people have a saying, "Tikkun Olam". It means heal the world, and it is one of the things I think is the most important part of creating new things in the world and spreading the wealth around to those who are having a not so great time.

This is the <u>only</u> thing you will ever do with your money that will give you a long-term sense that you are making a difference in the world.

Do not let that opportunity ever pass you buy. Contrary to what the world will tell you, you can only keep what you give away.

So, there you are, and there is my mission; to let every kid that steps through the door of the Sesula Mineral & Gem Museum get to experience the amazing world I work in, whether they are rich or poor, young or old. That is the true mission of the museum, and I still make great money doing it.

Notes